JENNY

Angela O'Hara

POOKA
BASEMENT PRESS
Dublin

DEDICATION

To my grandparents, Walter and Emily O'Hara and my mother Maureen, and to the beloved Canada of my childhood.

First published in 1995 by
Basement Press
an imprint of Attic Press
29 Upper Mount Street
Dublin 2

A Catalogue record for this title is available from the British Library
ISBN 185594 147 3

The moral right of Angela O'Hara to be identified as the Author of this Work has been asserted.

Basement Press would like to thank Microsoft Ireland for their support in the publication of this book.

Cover Illustration: Jon Donoghue
Cover Design: DanteBrisco
Origination: Attic Press
Printing: The Guernsey Press Co. Ltd

This book is published with the assistance of the Arts Council/An Chomhairle Ealaíon

Chapter One

Jenny stood in the laboratory, surrounded by the smell of carbolic soap and fermenting sesame seeds. The bright green linoleum-topped tables and glass beakers glittered in the very hot - too hot for the time of year - sun. On one of these shining green tables some very peculiar and highly secret experiments were taking place. Containers boiled and frothed with unimaginable liquids which ran through glass tubes into other containers containing boiling and frothing unimaginable liquids. All sorts of gauges and meters for calculating pressure, heat weight, density, and so on, were measuring these unimaginable boiling, frothing liquids. It was like a mad scientist's laboratory in the movies, and certainly everyone thought of Jenny's father as a mad scientist. But Jenny had grown up in strange surroundings and was well used to strange people and strange happenings. She thought that strange was quite normal.

Jenny herself was in the midst of scrubbing and cleaning the laboratory, and wore a blue plastic apron over her jeans, and a pair of black wellies that made a squelching noise when she walked on the tiled floor. She wasn't allowed to go anywhere near the brewing and sizzling experiments, but there was plenty of cleaning to be done elsewhere, and she knew she'd better get to it because her father was due back any time now. Nevertheless, she paused in her work to talk to a friend who was in a very bad mood and needed a good sorting-out.

'There's no point complaining to me, Twill,' said Jenny, picking up a red bucket lying on the floor and taking out the smelly mop that had become glued inside it. She filled the bucket up with water at the old-fashioned enamel sink. 'I've already spoken to my father and he refuses to let you out, even for a day. He says with this heat it would be dangerous.'

'But I can't stand it in here,' squeaked Twill. 'I can't stand small spaces - I have to get out - I'm going crazy in here. It's too hot - I'm suffocating - the walls are closing in on me! Eep-iddle-eep.'

'Oh, come on,' said Jenny. 'Remember the last time we let you out? You couldn't wait to get back in again. You said you were scared by all the wide spaces. I don't think I can put up with your ranting any more.'

'Well, that's obvious!' said Twill. Her little friend was short-legged and peevish and it didn't take much to get her feathers ruffled. 'I don't think you like me any more. You're more interested in some other bright-eyed fancy. You couldn't give a fig about me - I'm all alone - a prisoner - no one to love me! Twiddle-dee-dee!'

Jenny shook her head as she poured a handful of Cowbrand baking soda into the bucket. It

4

frothed and fizzed in the water. Baking soda was used for soap in the laboratory because it was biodegradable. Everything Jenny ate, wore, washed with and lived with was environmentally friendly. Especially her parents. Her father was the most environmentally friendly person she knew, though he was less than friendly when it came to fighting for the environment, and she was sure that a lot of people around would rather see him biodegrade than hear him preach any more about pollution.

Jenny's parents had met while her father was on sabbatical in Galway, Ireland. He had been studying the behaviour of the elusive corncrake, a very shy bird which makes its nests in cornfields. After he'd met her mother, a Connemara woman who spoke fluent Irish, her father had decided to stay in Ireland and bring up a family. The family had moved to Eastern Canada just two years before.

If you haven't already guessed, Jenny's father was an ornithologist. That is, he collected birds for a living - though he did study them as well. He was always involved in some crazy experiment or other.

Jenny had found Twill herself, lying with a broken wing at the bottom of a silver birch tree outside her house. Twill had fallen from her nest and was nearly half starved. Jenny knew that no chick could survive falling from a tree, because its mother would always abandon it. But she brought the chick back to her father's laboratory, anyway, and with her constant attention, Twill had been miraculously nursed back to health.

Ever since then, Jenny had been able to communicate with the robin. She didn't understand how. All she knew was that she understood what Twill was saying. Every movement, every sound she made, were like messages in some secret language. It was like magic. Not that she believed in magic. She lived in a strictly scientific world and everything in it could be explained scientifically. Except perhaps, this...

'Don't be stupid,' said Jenny now, opening Twill's cage to change the water in the water trough. 'You know you're the favourite around here, you little squirt. Why I put up with you at all -!'

'Watch out - you're splashing me!' cried Twill, jumping ba_k when the cold water splashed over her toes. She turned her little brown head to see one of the other inmates of the laboratory staring at her. 'What are you gawking at, you ugly brute?' Twill snapped, scratching her head with her foot. The brute looked away. 'Did you hear what he said to me? I tell you, they're a pack of bullies, all of them. They're trying to get me. I know it. They hate me!'

'That's just your imagination,' said Jenny. 'Here, I'll give you a piece of lettuce, if you're good.'

Twill shook her head in disgust. 'Do I look like I want a piece of lettuce?'

'You're tough to please,' said Jenny. 'Then how about some watercress or a big leaf of cabbage?

Too tough? Hard to chew, your highness? I know! An apple slice. I know you can't resist apple!'

This sounded definitely more interesting to Twill, who bobbed up and down in her cage in excitement at the idea of it. 'Give us apple! Give us apple!' she exclaimed.

Jenny heard the creak of the screen door behind her and when she turned around, she found herself looking at the placid face of her father's new research assistant, Louis, who had entered carrying a tray of slides.

'I saw you!' he said to Jenny. Beaming, he approached the cages of the birds. 'Now, how are my pretty pets today?'

'Saw me what?' Jenny asked, her face turning the colour of a boiled lobster. 'What did you see, Louis?'

'You were speaking to the bird again,' he said, opening a cage and feeding the yellow oriole a piece of grape from his fingers. The bird lapped up the fruit like a docile puppy. If it had had a tongue, it would have licked his hand.

'I - I wasn't speaking to the bird,' Jenny defended herself. 'I was talking to myself.'

'Well, now,' said Louis, setting down his tray on the table. 'If you were talking to that robin, that would have been fine. But now I know you were talking to yourself. That's another matter entirely. There must be something wrong with you.'

'You should know that people can't talk to birds,' Jenny said smartly.

7

Louis was one-half Micmac Indian, or so he said. The other half was supposed to have come from a French-Canadian woman from somewhere in Manitoba, a scientist who studied insects. Louis said he had grown up in a reserve not far from here where they hunted moose on snowmobiles and built totem poles.

However, strangely, no one in town seemed to have heard of Louis, and Jenny's father had never expected him to apply for this assistant's job, though he had been delighted when he had seen how wonderful Louis was with the birds. They seemed to sing more sweetly whenever Louis came into the room.

Louis was also extremely handsome. He was tall and finely featured and wore his long, raven-black hair flowing down the back of his white lab coat. His broad, serene face, hardly ever smiling, looked as if he knew something that she didn't, as if he had the whole answer to the universe in his pocket and was very smug about it.

Altogether, there was something very odd about Louis, though Jenny couldn't quite think what it was. It was as if he had one foot in her world and one foot somewhere beyond.

'Who says you can't talk to birds?' he asked her now, as he picked through a tray of dusty slides. 'It's possible if you have the gift.'

He was making fun of her! Her face hot with embarrassment, Jenny turned her back on him to clean the cage of a speckled nutcracker bird.

As she scraped, she stared out the glass windows, trying to ignore Louis' presence, which

8

she had decided was very distracting. She could see her mother's beautiful sunflowers through the window. They lolled and waved with the breeze, like big brown faces with frilly yellow bonnets. She wiped her forehead with her wrist and re-installed a wooden perch in a cage.

'You don't have to worry,' Louis said, digging in the rusty filing cabinet. 'I won't tell anyone. Your secret is safe with me.'

'What secret?' asked Jenny.

'That you talk to birds,' he replied.

'I don't talk to birds,' Jenny protested, emptying out her bucket of dirty water into the sink. 'I only talk to one bird.'

'I know,' said Louis. 'And the robin talks back to you.'

'How do you know -?' Jenny asked, surprised.

'There's no point in denying it,' Louis said. 'You have been given a gift. A very special gift. I've been watching you since I came here.' He sat down on an old wooden stool, smiling at her with his lovely, dark eyes. Louis always smiled with his eyes, never with his mouth, but it was always plenty for Jenny.

'Birds talk to us all the time,' he said, 'but that doesn't mean they can understand us or that we can understand them. Have you ever noticed a pet dog or cat? They will bark and mew at you to try to tell you something. Sometimes we listen to them, sometimes we don't. Mostly we don't. There are people like your father who will spend their whole lives trying to figure out what birds are saying to each other, while a special person will understand without any bother at all. This person has a gift. A lot of us are born with gifts but we lose them. And then we spend the rest of our lives trying to get them back. Your gift is understanding the language of birds.'

Behind them, the screen door swung open and Jenny's father burst into the room, his arms full of bundles of mail. 'Wonderful! You're still here, Louis,' Professor Wren said, letting the brown-paper parcels and envelopes topple on to his already overflowing desk. He gave Louis a mock salute. 'Mission accomplished!'

'Your expedition yesterday was successful, Professor?' Louis asked politely.

'Yes, yes. I hope the shots came out. I used a flash but it was so dim and I lost my glasses in the weeds,' Jenny's father said breathlessly as he pulled an envelope of photographs out of the breast pocket of his tattered tweed jacket. 'To think, African storks in our own Lake Omegod! I couldn't believe it when I heard the report. I had to go and see for myself. This will be wonderful for our case. So why are you still here, Louis? I thought you would have been gone home by now.'

'I was talking to your daughter.'

'Oh, of course. Jenny,' the professor said, as if suddenly remembering he had a daughter by that name. 'Well, I'm glad I caught you. You'll stay to dinner. I want you to take a gander at these photos. Come on, I'm starving.'

Chapter Two

Jenny's family was like a skittish butterfly on a windy afternoon. They were very hard to pin down. Her mother was a gardener and spent most of her time deep in the forest that surrounded Jenny's house, pulling up ladies' slippers and devil's paintbrushes, and other wild flowers. She was kind and gentle, but distant. Jenny always felt as if her mother thought of her as a seedling she had found in the woods, feeding her and watering her, watching her grow and develop with patience and a mild curiosity to see how Jenny would grow up.

Jenny's sister Alice was four years older and in her last year of high school. Jenny didn't see much of her, either. Alice was always out gallivanting with her friends and didn't spend any more time at home than she had to. Jenny's even older brother, Henry, studied business at the university. He was hardly ever to be seen at all, living and sleeping at his college campus and coming home only to be fed.

The Wrens all went about their business, hardly aware of each other. To catch sight of one during the day was like spotting a rare yellow-bellied sapsucker or a variegated woodpecker.

The only time Jenny's family would be found together was at suppertime. The squawking and chirruping that went on at the dinner table was deafening. Life at the Wrens' was a matter of survival of the fittest. The stronger chick will always gobble up all the food the parent brings, and the weaker will eventually starve and die. It sounds brutal, but that's the way Jenny saw it. In this case she wasn't fighting for food, but for attention. And Jenny felt like the weaker chick.

This evening they were having French-roast chicken, made with herbs that her mother had grown in her garden. It was a free-range chicken, if you could count running around in circles in their neighbour's backyard as free range. They also had scabby potatoes and carrots - organically grown, of course. The vegetables were scabby from the insects that ate them without fear of pesticides.

This was the first time Louis had stayed for dinner, and she did feel a little sorry for him in the chaos at the table.

'This is your domestic chicken,' Professor Wren announced, placing the platter on the table, 'developed for food production, free-range, of course. You can tell by the highly developed pectorals.' He pointed with his carving knife to the chicken breast and then to the drumsticks. 'And by the shapely quadraceps. This chicken got plenty of exercise. Mr Carson must have them running marathons. I hope you're not a vegetarian, Louis.'

'On no, I'm not a vegetarian,' Louis assured

him, watching Professor Wren hungrily as he tore off a large drumstick and put it on his plate.

'A lot of my colleagues are vegetarians,' said Jenny's father. 'But I can't resist my carnivore instincts, especially when I smell roast chicken.'

Louis nodded in appreciation as he chewed a chicken wing.

Jenny's father thought that they should have some atmospheric music as they dined, so he picked through his collection of tapes of bird sounds. 'In the waterfowl department, we have the blue heron, the whooping crane, the Canada goose, the kingfisher, terns, the wood duck, gannets, gulls, and everyone's favourite, loons. Yes, loons will do the trick.'

So, quite appropriately, Jenny's family ate their dinner to the lonely call of loons.

'Have some more fiddleheads, dear,' Mrs Wren said to Henry.

Fiddleheads were baby ferns or fernlings that hadn't unfurled yet and looked like the tops of fiddles. Jenny's mother collected them from the edge of the wood. They had a taste sort of between spinach and beet greens.

'Mother, you know I hate fiddleheads,' said Henry. 'Why can't we have something normal like frozen carrots or canned peas?'

'Fiddleheads are loaded with natural vitamins and minerals which are lost from vegetables that are commercially processed,' said Mrs Wren. 'And they put hair on your chest.'

'I have plenty of hair where I like it,' said Henry.

'The fiddleheads look big this year,' his mother said, spooning some on to her plate. 'More like cello-heads. Oh, Louis, I meant to tell you that my rosemary bush has made a miraculous recovery since you looked at it. It has completely turned over a new leaf.'

'Mother, I'm finished. Could I get some dessert?' asked Jenny.

'I am pleased to be of some help, Mrs Wren,' said Louis.

'I don't know how you do it, but you certainly have a gift,' she told him, reaching over to refill his wineglass. 'You're welcome in my greenhouse any time. Are you sure you won't have any more fiddleheads? I picked them myself.'

'No thank you, Mrs Wren,' said Louis. He looked over at Jenny and gave her a wink. 'One can get quite full on musical instruments.'

'Mother, I'm trying to tell you about my chemistry test,' said Alice. 'The first part was really hard but the second part was a piece of cake.'

'Did anyone mention cake?' asked Henry, looking around hungrily.

As the dinnertime chaos continued around her, Jenny watched, mesmerised, the circumnavigations of a suicidal hawk moth which was travelling around the flame of a candle in the middle of the table. She watched it as each time it circled the flame it got closer and closer until, finally, in one bright flash, it fell to the table, a sizzled crisp.

'We are always drawn to the flame,' Louis whispered to her as he picked up the burnt moth and closed his large hand around it. Then Jenny watched as Louis did something very strange.

He blew into his fist. As Jenny's family gabbled around them like a gaggle of noisy geese, a little miracle took place. When Louis opened his hand again, out flew the moth, perfect as before. It fluttered out of the dining room to circle the kitchen ceiling light. Jenny stared after it in amazement.

'You know, storks are fascinating birds surrounded by legend and superstition,' said Professor Wren, who had pulled out his photographs and spread them on the table before him.

'Don't people believe they deliver babies or something?' asked Henry.

'That's right. In Germany, it is believed that storks pluck babies from a well and then pinch the mother on the calf, which tells her to go to the hospital.'

'But why have they landed here?' asked Henry, who had started to gather up the dinner dishes. Thanks a lot, Henry, thought Jenny as she watched him escape to the kitchen. Leave everyone else to listen to one of her father's long, boring lectures.

'The wetlands of Europe, the stork's summer habitat, are drying up. The birds are looking for greener pastures,' Professor Wren explained. 'The only problem is that, while we have plenty of wetlands here for storks, the storks are not adapted to living in Canada. They don't know what to eat or where to build their nests. Our own food chain can hardly support our own wildlife, much less newcomers. For instance, Lake Omegod, which is home to a rich variety of wildlife, will become barren of any food for our birds or for storks if its waters continue to be polluted. That's why I'm fighting so hard to protect it.'

'Do you think the weather has anything to do with it?' Louis asked, politely refusing a bowl of ice-cream Alice offered him.

'Absolutely!' exclaimed Professor Wren. 'Look at the weather we're having. A heatwave in the beginning of March? It has to be affecting the birds' migratory patterns. The storks probably think they're flying to Spain. And it's all because of pollution! It's eating away the planet's natural defence system, the ozone layer. The ozone layer is kind of like the earth's skin, and once that is gone, we're pretty much vulnerable to anything that comes along. If we don't stop this pollution, the whole earth will become a desert and nothing will be able to live on it. Not even us.'

'Speaking of storks,' said Jenny's mother, cutting in before Professor Wren got too worked up, 'I got a letter from Brenda today. She had her baby - a boy!'

'Another baby?' asked Professor Wren, frowning.

'Yes, dear, the one she has been pregnant with for the last nine and a half months,' Jenny's mother explained.

n, that baby!'

ven though Brenda was Jenny's sister, she always thought of her as a distant relative. She saw her once a year, at most, when Jenny and her family made their annual trek up north for their summer vacation. Brenda lived in Thunderbay, Ontario, with her forester husband, Jeff, their three - now four - children, and a tribe of hungry mosquitoes the size of small woodchucks.

'I wonder if this new baby will grow up to be as big as his brothers and sisters,' said Alice, handing Henry her plate to be washed.

It was true that here in Canada, everything seemed to be on a larger scale. The flowers grew bigger and smelled sweeter. The sky seemed to go on for ever, and at night you could see the creamy smudge of white which was the Milky Way in its sparkling, star-filled depths. If you were lucky, you might even catch the glowing flash of white and blue of the *aurora borealis*, the Northern Lights. And it was true, children did grow bigger over here. Brenda's children were giants: huge, hardy, red-cheeked, and with the appetites of lumberjacks.

'I don't know,' said Professor Wren. 'They seem to defy everything I ever learned about genetics. What else does she say?'

'Well,' said Jenny's mother, 'they did a count of the salmon spawning in the river and it's definitely down from last year.'

'I could have told her that,' said Professor Wren, 'with that oil spillage over Christmas. But I wonder if that really is the cause. The world is

17

changing, Maura, and any time now we're going to have a disaster on our hands.'

Jenny wasn't surprised that her father would find the news about the salmon more interesting than the news about his new grandson.

'Louis,' he said excitedly now, 'have a look at these. Do you see anything odd in them?'

Louis took a couple of photographs from Professor Wren and peered at them. 'I see the storks,' he said, peering at one of the pictures. 'But what is this in the background?'

'The flash must have picked up the chrome. It's a large transport vehicle shielded by the trees,' said Jenny's father, his blue eyes wide and glittering brightly in the candlelight. 'What we have here is photographic evidence of the persons or company responsible for polluting Lake Omegod.'

'What are you going to do, Leo?' Jenny's mother asked anxiously. She didn't care for the look on her husband's face. She knew it could only mean trouble.

'But this is real proof and I intend to do something about it. I don't know what it is yet but I am going to do something.' He looked as if he meant it, too.

18

Chapter Three

The sky had that yellow-blue glaze of a hot summer night and the air was full of clouds of tiny flies that flew into your mouth if you kept it open too long. Jenny wandered into the garden to where Louis sat on one of the zigzag fences that zigged and zagged their way up and down along the garden path. These fences were made of old, hollow cedar logs and, before the invention of electric fencing, had been used by farmers. Now they were only rat-runs for chipmunks.

'The stars are like white blossoms, opening and closing their petals,' said Louis, staring up at the twinkles of the first stars of the evening.

'It is nice,' said Jenny. 'I am sorry about dinner. My family are kind of crazy.'

'I really enjoyed the chicken,' said Louis, smiling at her. 'It's been a long time since I sat down to a home-cooked meal. I've been on the road a lot lately.'

'You know, that was really amazing what you did with the moth at the dinner table.' The more she thought about it, in fact, the more amazed she became. 'How did you do it?'

'Oh, just a little sleight-of-hand trick I picked

up from an old friend of mine.' Louis looked over to Jenny. Perhaps it was just the reflection of the scenery around her, but she could clearly see mountains and forests in the depths of his eyes. It was eerie.

They sat against the fence for a while, staring up into the heavens.

'Louis,' asked Jenny, suddenly. 'Do you think birds have souls?'

'Everything has a soul,' said Louis.

A stupid question to ask Louis, Jenny thought to herself. She knew from school that Native Indians believed that everything - rocks, water, trees - had a soul. She wanted to ask Louis about what he had said earlier that afternoon. She wanted to ask him about her gift. 'Louis, you said that people lose their gifts when they get older. Why?'

'Well,' said Louis, crossing his arms and looking thoughtful. 'A gift is like a muscle. It has to be exercised, kept in tune. An artist must paint, a musician must practise. If they don't, their muscle will turn to flab and, with time, just fade away.'

'But why would anyone just let it fade away?' asked Jenny.

'Because,' said Louis, taking a sip of his wine, 'they don't believe in their gifts. They don't use them to do the good for which they were intended. Other things get in the way as they get older. Then they forget all about them.'

'What can I do to keep mine?' Jenny was determined to do all she could not to let her gift fade away.

'You will have to use it for something important,' he said, lowering his voice to a whisper as if it was a very important secret. 'Something that will change the world. Do it before it's too late. I will tell you an old Micmac tale. There once was a man who was a great tracker and the whole village relied on him to track the caribou herds. Now, one day, the tracker had been travelling over the fields and hills and mountains for days looking for caribou, and he was exhausted and hungry from his journey. At last he saw a caribou. He knew that if there was one caribou, there were a hundred caribou. But he decided to take rest in the shade of an old oak tree. But he fell fast asleep! When he woke up, he discovered that he had slept all day and all night and now it was the morning of the next day. The robin was singing in the tree but the caribou were gone. He searched for days for them, but they left no trail.'

'Where did they go?' asked Jenny. 'The caribou?'

'They just disappeared,' said Louis. 'The hunter lost his chance.'

'But that wouldn't have been the only caribou in the world, would it?' asked Jenny. 'More caribou would come along.'

'Not for the tracker,' said Louis, shaking his head sadly. 'He and most of his village starved to death that winter.'

'Oh,' said Jenny, surprised by the frightening ending of what she thought was just a harmless little story. 'But I can't see how I could make any difference.'

'You have a great gift,' said Louis. 'The ability to talk to birds.'

'I wish I was a bird,' said Jenny, staring up at the stars. She expected him to laugh at her, but he didn't. 'If I was a bird, I would fly away from this place. No school, no family. I would be free ...'

'Are you sure that's what you want?' asked Louis, looking at her steadily.

They were interrupted by her father, who had returned from the lab with a book about storks which he wanted to show Louis under his arm.

'Yes,' said Jenny strongly. 'That's what I want.'

That night, Jenny went to bed late. It was twelve o'clock. She couldn't wait for next week. Next week was March Break, a whole week of holidays. Jenny looked up at her calendar, which was illustrated with a photograph of a lighthouse from Prince Edward Island.

She rolled open the large window in her bedroom. Outside, the night was heavy and moist with heat. It was absolutely still. She could hear the comforting chirp of crickets and see the occasional glowing flight-path of a passing firefly. As she stared out into the inky darkness, alive with night sounds, she thought of what Louis had said. She wondered how she could use her gift, how she could change the world. What could she do? She was only a thirteen-year-old girl and it was a tall order. Besides, what could she do for the world that her father was not already doing?

That night Jenny had a dream. It was a dream much like those she had had many times before. She dreamt she was flying, high over the trees and fields and lakes. Everything looked tiny below. She was swooping and diving. She could feel the breeze against her face and the scent of the trees and fields below her.

But something was different about this dream. In the other dreams, she felt at peace, happy to be alive and free, sailing through the sky, high over the world, away from everything and everyone. But in this dream, she was frightened. Something was chasing her, making her fly faster than ever before. She narrowly missed flying into the weather vane her neighbours, Mr and Mrs Macguire, had on the top of their house. She just missed the spiky spines of a pine tree. She couldn't see what was chasing her, but she was terrified. She feared for her life and whatever it was that was chasing her was getting closer and closer. She just couldn't fly fast enough to get away.

Jenny woke in the middle of the night feeling sticky with sweat and very afraid.

Chapter Four

When Jenny entered the laboratory, she was confronted by a very strange-looking man.

He was short and stubby and wore a tweed jacket with leather patches on the elbows. He had a big, beaky nose and beady black eyes that missed nothing as they scanned her father's laboratory like a hawk. Jenny distrusted him instantly.

'And who is this now?' The man peered at Jenny as if he was staring at an insect on a pin.

'This is my daughter, Jenny,' said Professor Wren. 'Jenny, this is Professor Mennis, a scientist from Queens University who has come down especially to meet me.'

Professor Mennis's smile was like a snarl. Jenny would have preferred it if he'd kept his smiles to himself.

Jenny's father showed Professor Mennis around the lab, waving his arms about with enthusiasm as he showed him his favourite specimens and talked about his experiments in bird language. Professor Mennis followed quietly behind, gazing sharply at everything around him.

'And I believe,' said Professor Wren excitedly,

'that there's a pattern in all bird songs. I want to prove that birds of different species can communicate, and that perhaps we can learn their language! This is the rare orange flycatcher. He comes from these parts. They're almost extinct.'

'This is a very fine bird,' said Professor Mennis, looking into a cage that contained a large crow. Jenny thought that they certainly looked alike with their beaky noses, small beady black eyes, and bad-humoured scowl. 'What is it?'

'A carrion crow I brought from Ireland,' said Jenny's father. 'They very rarely kill anything themselves; they feed off the carrion and waste left behind by other predators.'

'Someone has to clean up the mess,' said Professor Mennis. He looked at Jenny, smiling. 'A noble creature, isn't it, my dear? And what is this?' he asked, peering into Twill's small cage.

'Oh, that's just a common robin, a pet. Jenny found it when it was a chick. It had fallen from its nest. She nursed it back to health. Any day it should be let back out into the wild. Quite wonderful, really.'

Jenny was surprised her father remembered what she had done for Twill. She was also surprised that Professor Mennis, an ornithologist, couldn't recognise a common robin when he saw one.

Professor Mennis stuck one of his long, pointy fingers into Twill's cage. Twill, clearly taking a dislike to this man and his finger, promptly gave him a sharp little nip.

25

'Oww! Oh! Did you see that? The little gnat bit my finger,' howled Professor Mennis, sucking his wounded digit. 'If I get my hands on that scrawny pencil neck, I'll - I'll -' He curled his lips up into another awful smile. 'He's a perky little fellow, isn't he?'

'Are you all right?' asked Jenny's father. 'Let me put some iodine on that bite.'

'N-n-no, it's just fine. I'll heal. Tell me, Professor Wren. I hear you're a bit of an environmental activist. I heard you on the radio. You have some pretty strong views.'

'Well, someone has to,' said Professor Wren, 'or nothing will get done. It will be too late before the government gets their act in gear.'

'You mentioned that you might have information about the pollution of Lake Omegod,' said Professor Mennis. 'Do you know who might be responsible?'

'I do have a few leads,' said Jenny's father.

'What do you plan to do?' asked the visitor.

'I don't know yet,' her father admitted, giving him a curious look.

Professor Mennis continued to interrogate her father about Lake Omegod. But Jenny's father had stopped answering the questions. He was suspicious, too.

The strange professor said he had to leave for an appointment in the city. Jenny was pleased to see the back of him. There was something wrong about him, something rotten. She could nearly smell it off him.

Chapter Five

The flagstone path to the laboratory was framed by cedar fences, and the bitter but pleasant smell of marigolds and chrysanthemum that had been in bloom since February filled the air. The sun was shining hard and strong, and she was glad of the straw hat and sunglasses her mother had made her put on. A dragonfly droned by.

Today was the first day of March Break and Jenny was delighted. She hated school. She hated being told what she should learn. Her father and mother had a huge library of books on everything, and she couldn't imagine school teaching her anything that wasn't in those books. And Jenny had plenty of time to read them, too. Ever since she had moved from Galway two years before, she had found it very difficult to make new friends. Or no one else at school seemed very interested in making friends with her. But she didn't mind. At least, she told herself she didn't mind.

Her father's laboratory was a circular building made of wood. It looked something like a gazebo, except that all the empty bits were filled in with glass and screens. Her mother had planted the tall, waving sunflowers, nearly six foot high, to hide the gawkiness of the building.

All the fruit trees in the front garden were in full blossom. In the middle of this orchard was an old, gnarled cherry tree where birds could be singing merrily, day in and day out. Jenny always loved this tree. It reminded her of a tale from the *Arabian Nights*, 'The Singing Tree', about a princess who goes in search of the three most wonderful things in the world: the golden water, the talking bird, and the singing tree, a tree that sang continuously with sweet voices. Ever since she had read this tale, she always thought of this beautiful old cherry tree as the Singing Tree.

There were at least a hundred bird feeders planted throughout her mother's garden. Now Jenny came up to one made from a red-stained timber and built to look like a Swiss chalet. It was triangular and had a chimney and a balcony. Jenny thought of the chickadees reclining on the balcony with their cigars, or maybe grilling seeds on a tiny barbecue, and smiled. She scooped birdseed out of the bucket into the bird feeder, and moved on to the next one.

As she filled the feeder, she saw something move in her mother's flowerbeds. Two very long ears poked out of the delphiniums. Then a brown hare leaped out of the flowers and on to the path. The creature stared at her for a long moment before loping lazily down the path away from her. Then, with one leap, it was over the cedar zigzag fence and had disappeared into the tangled shelter of bushes beyond.

What a bold creature, Jenny thought to herself,

just sitting there like that and brazenly staring at me. But there had been something unsettling in the hare's direct gaze. It had seemed to look straight through her. Probably just her imagination, she thought, and she turned back to her task.

'Hey, Jenny!'

She saw her neighbour, Blake, running towards her down the path. Blake lived across the road with his three brothers and his Baptist parents. He was one of the cutest boys in her class, but she didn't trust him one inch. 'Oh hi, Blake,' she said, hardly looking at him.

He was dressed in jeans and a blue T-shirt with a transfer on it that spelled out the letters WWF, interlaced with a little yellow bird.

'What's that badge?' asked Jenny sourly. 'World Wrestling Federation?'

'No,' said Blake. 'It's the World Wildlife Trust. Your father gave us and all the group a badge on that nature walk he took us on.'

'Oh, how nice,' she said, mockingly.

'I thought you might have gone on the nature walk, too,' said Blake.

'What, on one of those walks?' Jenny laughed bitterly. 'Forget it! I'd die of boredom! All that nature!'

'It was pretty interesting,' said Blake, watching her as she scooped the seed from the bucket with probably more energy than was needed, sending a spray of poppy seed over the begonias.

'Why did you come here anyway?' asked Jenny. 'Can't you see I have work to do?'

'I came to ask you if you wanted to go on a hike, but I can see that you're busy,' said Blake, becoming irritated with Jenny's tone.

'Yes, I am busy,' she snapped. 'Unlike some people, I have chores to do. Why don't you go and ask Michelle Curry? Isn't she your girlfriend? I'm sure she'd love to go on a hike with you.'

'She's not my girlfriend. Besides, I came to ask you,' he said. 'But I guess I've made a mistake.'

'Yes, you have,' she said sharply. 'Goodbye then.'

'Fine!' he huffed. 'Goodbye.' He went to turn away and was halfway down the path when he turned and shouted, 'Jenny Wren, you have to be the crabbiest person I know. This will be the last time I come over to see you!'

'Fine!' shouted Jenny, not even looking up at him. 'And good riddance!'

Jenny's face was hot with anger as she stomped towards the laboratory. Why did he even bother to come over? I'm just a standby to him, a convenient person to waste a couple of hours with when he is bored. Just because she lived down the road didn't mean she was there for whenever he felt like a bit of company. He had some nerve!

'I don't care if I never see him again!' she exclaimed to herself.

The laboratory was empty. Louis was nowhere to be seen. She called him but she got no answer. He'll be back soon, no doubt, she thought, and went straight to Twill's cage. She suddenly felt that she needed a friend.

'I don't play second fiddle to anyone with you, do I?' she said to Twill.

'Well, that's true, that's true,' cried Twill.

Jenny went into one of the lab refrigerators. She pulled off a leaf of lettuce and squished it into Twill's cage.

'That man - that man,' said Twill.

'What man?' asked Jenny, putting on her plastic apron.

'That professor - that professor - he's bad - he's -'

Jenny heard the dull click of the screen door opening behind her. Holding her breath and with a thumping heart, she slipped into the closet with the brooms and camera tripods and put her eye to a crack in the door to see who had come in.

It was the stubby, tweed-clad body of Professor Mennis! She should have known, she thought to herself. She had felt that there was something very wrong about him. Should she jump out and surprise him? She decided to stay in her hiding place and see what he was up to.

Chapter Six

From Jenny's hiding place in the closet, she could see the professor scuttling around like a cockroach, peeking into this and looking under that. He pulled huge bunches of files from the filing cabinet and rifled through them. Some he stuffed into his leather briefcase, but the rest he left scattered all over the floor.

'Now where would he keep them?' Jenny could hear him grumbling as he searched. 'Where would someone hide something if they wanted to keep it very secret?'

Professor Mennis was leaving an awful mess. A trail of trampled papers and files, photographic negatives and slides was left behind him as he ploughed through one drawer after another. Through the crack in the cupboard door, Jenny saw him make his way over to the green linoleum table with her father's lab equipment. There was a loud crash as he knocked over a couple of the glass containers holding some of the unimaginable liquids.

Then she heard him say something very strange.

'What would you do if you were me?' she heard him ask. 'I wish I could be you and have those sharp eyes. I'd find what I want in no time. What? You say look in that drawer? Why, thank you my dearest, I will. I can see that you and I are from the one stock.'

Who could he be talking to? She heard another loud crash as another glass container struck the tiled floor. This time the crash was followed by a yelp. Professor Mennis must have hurt himself, she thought.

A few moments passed and she could hear nothing. Something sharp was sticking between her shoulderblades and it was becoming more and more uncomfortable. Jenny held her breath and tried to change her position while holding on to the knob of the closet door. But shifting in such an awkward place was a mistake and as soon as she moved, a broom handle fell forward against the door with a loud clattering sound that resounded through the laboratory.

Jenny thought her heart would leap out of her chest.

Through the crack in the door she could see Professor Mennis's beady little eyes darting around in search of whatever had caused the noise. She saw him take something slowly out of his inside jacket pocket. It was a big, ugly gun. It was silver and cold, and heartless.

He approached the cupboard door, gun poised. Jenny froze with fear. But then suddenly she heard a voice that she knew all too well.

'Come over here, you ugly mug,' Twill shrieked at the top of her little voice. 'Come over here. Put up your dukes, you phoney.'

Professor Mennis's eyes swivelled towards Twill's cage. Did he understand Twill? Jenny saw him stare at the cage. Twill said nothing but made loud birdish noises, and bounced up and down on her perch.

Professor Mennis shook his head and stepped towards the cupboard again. Jenny was sure he had seen her. She had felt his cold gaze looking straight at her. It was like the cold air that rushes out of the freezer when you open the door. Jenny shivered.

'I know you're in there, my pretty.' Professor Mennis's voice was as sweet as molasses and just as unpleasant. 'I can see you. No one is here, just you and me and the birdies. You better come out now.'

The phone rang, shattering the tension.

The screen door banged closed and then there was silence. All the tripods and brooms came down with a crash as Jenny burst out of the cupboard and tried to reach the phone. It stopped ringing just as she grabbed the receiver.

Her heart was pounding so hard, she had to take a couple of long, deep breaths. She looked around at the laboratory. Professor Mennis had overturned the whole room. It was a frightening mess.

She tiptoed through the scattered files and the broken slides and bottles. Numbly, she started to clean up the mess. What could that vulture have been looking for? she wondered to herself as she picked up the files and put them back into the cabinet. They would be all out of order, she knew, but it was the best she could do for the moment.

What was her father going to say when he found out that there was a little more to this Professor Mennis than met the eye? He was probably a spy sent from some nuclear power plant or some company which dumped chemicals into the lake late at night. It was probably a big conspiracy. They probably thought her father had information that could blow the whole top off the thing. Obviously 'Professor Mennis' had come to make sure that didn't happen. One look at that gun he had in his hand told Jenny that the strange man would do whatever he had to do in order to stop her father. For the first time Jenny realised the danger her father was in.

There was a small, rectangular piece of card sitting among the debris. Professor Mennis must have dropped it when he was looking through the drawers. This must be his business card, Jenny thought. Now she would find out who this Professor Mennis really was. And she would go to the police and tell them everything.

She read the card aloud:

Acid Drops & Lollipops, Inc.
Producers of quality goodies,
chocolates, after-dinner wafers and breathmints
for the discerning tastebuds.

Sedric Hawkings
Marketing manager.

'Acid Drops & Lollipops? What kind of name is

that for a nuclear power plant?' No, it must be some mistake. Could Sedric Hawkings be Professor Mennis's real name?

She tried to phone her father's work number but the secretary said he had already left. She would have to wait. She wondered again where Louis was. It was very strange that he should be away for so long.

All she could do was wait and clean up the mess the fake Professor Mennis had left behind him. She bent down to pick up a pile of folders on the floor.

'Ow!' she cried and dropped the files. Her finger was bleeding - and then she saw the piece of broken glass. There was a fragment stuck in her finger.

When she looked down, she saw that a small glass tube had been broken. A deep purple liquid had spilled over the floor. It reminded Jenny of something one would spread on pancakes. It fizzed a little when she moved it, sparkling in the sun. Jenny stuck her wounded finger into her mouth. The purple liquid tasted sweet, like grape soda.

'I know that whatever this stuff is, it's probably something that can either turn me blue or burn my insides out. I hope I haven't poisoned myself.'

Twill stared at her from her cage with her black, unblinking eyes.

'I feel strange,' said Jenny, holding her forehead. 'Sort of all fizzy. My head feels light, like a balloon.' She sort of felt like grape soda herself, now.

Twill wavered a bit on her perch but was silent.

'What's happening?' cried Jenny. The image of Twill was shuddering in front of her. She thought she was going to faint. It must be the fright or the heat or both, she told herself as the laboratory began to blur and twirl around her like a merry-go-round until she gratefully faded into blackness.

It was then that she had her strange dream again. She was flying out of the lab and into the brilliant blue sky. She was swooping and swerving high over the hills and trees, over dense, cool forests of firs and spruce trees, pines bent crooked by wind. She flew over apple orchards heavy with pink blossoms. She could smell the blossoms. They were sweet and refreshing. She flew over rivers and streams, over the headpond at the bottom of the hill where she lived, where the beavers built their dams. She flew over fields of freshly tilled soil ready for sowing. The sky, a brilliant silvery blue, was shimmering. The sun was a blurry yellow ball.

Jenny could see her house, its shingled roof and chimney. She could see the garden and all the bird feeders. As she flew on, she saw her mother at the edge of the forest, digging up a clump of blue wild irises with her spade. Jenny tried to call to her, but her voice sounded funny, more like a squeak. Her throat felt tight, her tongue dry.

A butterfly fluttered by her and she suddenly wanted to catch it. She flew after it, pushing against the cool breeze.

She was flying downwards now, towards the funny gazebo building that housed her father's laboratory. She was flying towards the leaning sunflowers. They seemed to wave at her, beckon to her. She was flying straight towards their brown pebbly faces like a dart at a bull's-eye.

Then she woke up and discovered it was not a dream.

Chapter Seven

'Oh, no!' Jenny cried, swerving and listing drunkenly, first to one side and then the other, before landing headlong into a clump of stinging nettles. 'Ouch!' She slowly pulled out the nettle needle that was sticking into her toe. 'Oh, my foot, I think I broke it! I am never going to try that again. It's bad for my health.'

Moaning with pain, she flopped clumsily out of the bed of nettles and on to the lawn beyond. Once she was on the lawn, she had a difficult time seeing through the long, shifting blades of glass that were taller than her head.

I thought Henry had cut this grass, she thought to herself. I can hardly see through it. This has to be the strangest dream I have had yet.

It certainly was a very real dream. Well, she might as well take inventory, she told herself, and brace herself for any surprises. She had wings, that was for certain, so she must be a member of the bird family. But what kind?

Just ahead of her on the lawn was a concrete birdbath in the shape of a scallop shell. With very little effort, she was able to hop on to the ledge and peer into the bath's still surface.

'Mirror, mirror in the well,' she said, 'who's the

fairest on this shell?'

Her reflection shimmered glassily under a light breeze, but when it was stilled, there was no denying the image. She couldn't possibly understand how but someone, something, had stolen her arms and legs and left her with this scrawny, feather-decked little body. Somehow, some way, she had been changed into a small variegated song bird of the robin variety.

Yes, yes, it's true, she thought to herself. There was no denying it. She was indeed a robin. She wasn't certain if this was a dream or the real thing. Maybe this isn't even happening to me at all, she thought. I could have taken something that makes you see things that aren't there. I could be hullabaloo-cinating. But the concrete shell under her feet felt real, and so did the hot sun beating down on her little pea-sized head.

Suddenly, a colossal bumblebee flew by and Jenny was nearly toppled off the birdbath by the breeze created by its wings. It felt like a giant transport truck roaring by her. The bumblebee hummed a tune to itself as it bumbled along, and it deafened Jenny's sensitive ears.

'Hey, watch where you're going, you - you insect!' she squawked, beating her wings angrily. 'And leave the singing to us birds!'

Well, one thing was for certain, she was a great deal smaller than she used to be and everything else was a great deal bigger. The bird houses that surrounded her in the garden looked like a vast, cluttered metropolis on stilts. The daisies and yellow chrysanthemums were as big as trees, and the trees were as big as skyscrapers.

Sitting there on that scallop shell for everyone and their pets to see, she suddenly felt very small and insecure. She wanted to fly to the Singing Tree and sit on that big, gnarled branch, the low one, all curved and wrinkled like a reptile's tail. She could just imagine the wonderful feeling of sitting there, protected from the strong heat and sun, nearly drunk on the perfume of its pink cherry blossoms.

But now how was she to get there? Another attempt at flight could be perilous. But if she stayed here any longer, she would be roast robin.

'I can do this,' she said. 'I think I can, I think I can.' She launched herself awkwardly off the shell and into the air. Her body was so light that the force of the breeze pushed her this way and that. Instead of flapping, she tried to straighten her wings and glide, but things flew past so fast that they made her dizzy. She just kept going down and down like a jet plane missing the runway and making a crash lansding - in her case in a bramble bush at the base of the cherry tree.

'Oh, not again!' Jenny groaned. She tried to pull herself out of the brambles and find where all the bits of her were, which was pretty difficult as she was upside down. After a little time she managed to right herself, and a few attempts later, she made it to the gnarled branch of the cherry tree.

The cherry tree was like a world unto itself of interlacing leaves, twigs, and branches, buzzing

41

with insect life and the chatter of squirrels and chipmunks. Jenny had always loved climbing, and had tree-houses in many trees around the house. She always enjoyed the shady solitude within their branches, far away from the loneliness of the house. She could always think well in a tree, too, it was so peaceful there. But she had never thought she would actually have to live in a tree.

'Are you hurt, hurt, hurt?' An unfamiliar voice came from above her, from somewhere above within the scented petals of the cherry tree. She peered through the foliage for the owner. However, there was no person on the lawn.

'I'm right here, here, here.' Now the voice was beside her but all she could see were leaves and branches and a tiny black and white bird. 'That wasn't a pretty sight, sight, sight. You must be hurt, hurt, hurt from your crash. Was something trying to eat you? I say, you made a brave escape.'

There was no question about it, the little black and white bird was talking to her.

Another voice came from the shelter of the tree. 'Who are you talking to down there, Rosehip?'

'A stranger, ger, ger,' said Rosehip. 'Come down and see for yourself.'

In a flash, another bird landed on the branch. It was a robin, just like herself. 'Hello there,' said the robin. 'Parley-vous English? You're new around here, aren't you? It's obvious to see you're new around here. Plain as day, clear as a

42

bell, you're new around here.'

'Yes, or no, I think so,' said Jenny. Her voice came out as a sharp twitter. She looked furtively around, wondering where the twitter came from. It couldn't possibly have come from her.

'There's not much you seem to know. You must have a concushin, or may be amnesier. Yes, you must have amnesier. Well, permit me to introduce myself,' said the robin. 'My name is Peat, and this is Rosehip. Can you remember your name?'

'Oh, I'm -' she started, still a little shocked by the sound of her own voice, 'I'm Jenny.'

'Are you sure you're all right, Jenny?' asked the other robin. 'You're not suffering from any post-romantic shock? You look a little grey around the gills, reddish about the breast, and generally a nasty and unhealthy shade of brown.'

Jenny looked at her feathers. She didn't see anything particularly out of the ordinary about them. If she was a robin, she was a robin and this was the colour she was supposed to be. 'I don't think I come in any other colour,' she said. 'Though I do feel a little ill. My stomach is full of butterflies.'

'Oh, you just had dinner,' said Peat. 'Well, don't worry. You're just suffering from a little indigestion.'

Well, at least one thing was for certain, thought Jenny, her father was right about birds communicating with each other.

'So what brings a nice-looking bird to this neck of the woods, anyway?' said Peat, shyly. 'You're

43

not waiting for your mate, perchance, perhaps, per tetre, maybe?'

'My what?' asked Jenny, not sure she had heard him correctly. In fact, she wasn't too sure she heard anything Peat said correctly. He said everything in fast-forward.

'I can't believe you're using that old line, line, line,' said Rosehip. 'That's as old as my granny.'

'I can ask, can't I?' said Peat irritably, glaring at her. 'That's not breaking any laws, is it?'

'It could be, be, be,' said Rosehip, and then turned to Jenny. 'Have you found a place to roost yet, yet, yet?'

'I've always liked this tree,' said Jenny.

'This is a fine tree, a delightful tree, a tree and a half,' exclaimed Peat with gusto. 'Are you sure you're not engaged or anything?'

'You seem to be very keen about getting married,' said Jenny.

'I have had ten wives,' said Peat proudly.

'Ten wives, huh!' said Rosehip scornfully.

'Ten wives!' exclaimed Jenny. 'Why do you want so many wives?'

'I don't have them all at once,' Peat said indignantly. 'What do you take me for? A pigamist? I have one wife a year,' he said. 'Two in a good season. But I haven't found my beloved yet this year and it's getting late - late for a very important date.'

'What's all the racket down there?' another voice boomed from above. 'Can't you see I'm trying to sleep?'

Peat looked above him. 'Oh Legenhazit, come

down here and see who I've found.'

With a flutter of tawny feathers, the little owl landed beside Jenny, Peat and Rosehip on the thick, knotty branch. 'All I ask for is a little peace and quiet,' said the Acadian bard owl. 'And all I get is chatter, chatter, chatter.'

'This is Toadflax,' said Rosehip, 'though everyone calls him Legenhazit.'

'Why do you call him that?'

'Because he is always saying "Legend has it, legend has it." Toadflax is our resident story-teller,' Rosehip told her. 'He's not too welcome in these parts. The council is always trying to get rid of him. They say he's bad for our morals, whatever that is.'

'A moral,' said Peat authoritatively, 'is something like your liver or stomach, and we always seem to be upsetting it. It must be like eating a bad worm. If we do anything we're not supposed to do, like listen to one of Toadflax's stories, we'll get a pain in our moral.'

Jenny giggled to herself. She told Peat that she thought lots of people got a pain there from time to time.

Chapter Eight

Jenny was delighted with all the new characters she met that day. Rosehip, the chickadee, was clever and always had a quick remark to hand. Toadflax was very kind and knew hundreds of stories, like 'How the Skunk Got Its Stripes' and 'How the Beaver Got Its Tail'. He knew just about everything there was to know about these woods. But of all the birds Jenny met, it was Peat she felt closest to. He was funny, and always had an explanation for everything. He took her under his wing and delighted in showing her all the tricks of the trade.

That afternoon she also met Juniper, the redwinged blackbird, who was very melodramatic at times; Speedwell, the swallow who lived in her next-door neighbour's barn but liked to sit in the tree to get away from 'the wife'; Bud the sparrow and his mates, who were chatty and friendly but not too clever; Hyacinth, who was over on holidays from the Canary Islands; and Bruno and Olio, who had emigrated from southern Italy.

And then there was Old Hornbeam, the great grey owl. Old Hornbean lived at the very top of the cherry tree and kept watch for predators during the night. Jenny never got a chance to meet him, but then very few of the birds in the Singing Tree had, because he slept all day and no one dared disturb his rest. They were afraid he would fly away to another tree and they wouldn't have his protection. But he was supposed to be very wise. Some said that he even had the ability to see into the future. But he was also rumoured to have an awful temper - they said that he ate little songbirds, though no one had actually seen him do it.

There were so many other birds living in the cherry tree that Jenny couldn't remember all their names. But they were very friendly, and they all had their story to tell. Iris and Columbine, two woodpigeons, were very proud of their new egg and liked to talk to Jenny about their domestic life.

'That husband of mine is never back on time,' said Columbine. 'I've been waiting all day for a bite to eat. Do you think it's easy sitting on an egg all day? I tell you, it's boring. I didn't even want an egg, at first. But you know that husband of mine. Every year at springtime, he wants an egg and sulks and sulks until he gets it. Now, I'm the one that's stuck here all day, with nothing, not even a crossword, while that husband of mine is off gallivanting with his cronies. Is that typical or is that typical?'

'I, I -' said Jenny.

'But you must look at my egg,' said Columbine. 'It is a beauty! To see it is to love it. Once I have my egg, it's the same old story. I can think of nothing else, wondering and dreaming of the hatching. I can't wait for him to pop.'

'How do you know it will be a male chick?' asked Jenny.

'How? Well, that's simple. When you drop the egg, you can tell by the way it falls. If the egg points to the north, it will be a male. If the egg points to the south, it will be a female. It's quite simple.'

Mossy, the greenfinch hen, had a different story. 'Every year, I pick a brand-new husband. What do I look for in a husband? Well, I like a good provider. He should know where to find the best grubs and plenty of them. He should be a skilful nestbuilder and be able to find good twigs to make a strong nest. But most of all, he should be a good conversationalist. I mean, dearie, when you are stuck together for a whole season, you have to find things to talk about, or it can be very awkward.'

All afternoon the birds chatted and sang and made merry and told stories. Jenny had never felt so much a part of everything. She was almost embarrassed by all the attention she was getting.

The unbearable heat of the afternoon was now draining into a pleasant evening. A lovely orange sunlight tipped the Kenwick Mountain, bathing everything in its warm glow. The birds of the Singing Tree began their chorus of evening song to bid farewell to the sun and celebrate the end of another day.

From the sheltered embrace of the Singing Tree, Jenny felt safe as she looked over the warm evening. The trees formed softly vibrating silhouettes like gentle giants keeping nightwatch over the woodland animals. The evening was alive with night sounds and smells. Above, the sky was clear, the stars shone bright and close. Jenny could see perfectly the constellation of the Big Dipper.

'Do you know the story of how the robin got its red breast?' asked Toadflax, landing softly beside her on the branch.

'Oh, Toadflax,' said Jenny, starting at his unexpected landing. 'I didn't hear you coming up behind me. No. I've never heard the story.'

'Do you see up there?' Toadflax indicated with his wing the constellation Jenny knew as the Big Dipper. 'That's the Bear.'

'The Bear?' asked Jenny.

'Yes, those four stars are the Bear, and the other stars following the bear are the Chickadee, the Robin and the Moosejay, and that little faint star is the Chickadee's pot where she will cook the meat.

'At this time of year, the bear awakes from her long sleep and starts to search for food. It is believed by those who will believe it that one day when the world was new, the Chickadee saw a bear coming out of its den and decided to hunt it. But the Chickadee was too small to hunt the bear all by herself, so she asked the Robin and Moosejay, Bluejay and Pigeon, and two Owls to help her.

'Now, through the summer the Bear flees from her hunters across the northern horizon. When

49

autumn comes, those who are slowest lose their way, one by one, until only Robin, Chickadee and Moosejay are left in the chase. Finally, it's the middle of the autumn and the three birds catch the bear and Robin pierces her with her arrow. Robin is so thin and hungry by this time that she dives right into the bear and gets covered with blood. She tries to shake off all the blood and the drops fall off to the earth and stain the forests below. That is why the trees turn red and orange in mid-autumn, especially the maple tree, which caught most of the blood.

'The first time they caught the Bear Robin managed to shake off all the blood but one spot on her breast, which wouldn't come off.

'"You will have that spot for as long as your name is Robin," said the chickadee. And that is why the robin has a red breast, or so legend has it,' said Toadflax.

'What about the bear?' asked Jenny.

'Well, every spring there is another bear and the hunt begins anew. It's a never-ending story.'

'Toadflax remembers all the stories of days gone by,' said Peat. 'He would keep you up all night telling you stories, wouldn't you, Toadflax? Just don't let the Council hear you or they'll have you tarred and defeathered.'

'I don't care what the Council does. Someone has to preserve our stories and legends,' said the little bard owl passionately, 'or they will all be lost.'

'I think they're wonderful stories,' said Jenny.

It was beginning to get quite dark and it was

far past the time that birds should be up. As all the tenants of the Singing Tree preened their feathers and prepared for bed, Columbine took Jenny aside to give her a few pieces of friendly advice. She told Jenny that she had to be as quiet as a mouse and never stir so as to avoid attracting predators.

'Old Hornbeam is here to protect everyone who lives in this tree,' said Columbine. 'But when he goes hunting he's not here to warn us with his hooting. Sometimes birds disappear from this tree, stolen in the night by the predators. We can never be too careful. So we have to be very quiet.'

Jenny huddled in between Peat and Rosehip. There was only a slip of a moon and the night was deep. Jenny suddenly felt a thrill up her spine. Columbine's words had spooked her, it was true, but this was more than that. She felt as if someone or something was watching her. She felt its eyes boring into her through the darkness. She shuddered at every movement around her. Every tremor of every blade of glass, every waggle of every leaf, every whir of a passing insect was a threat.

Now Jenny understood why the other birds slept with their heads under their wings, and she quickly followed their example.

Chapter Nine

It was dawn and the sun was floating softly above the headpond as if it, too, was too lazy to rise and face the day. The birds were just beginning to wake up and prepare for their morning songs. Jenny had barely opened her eyes when there was a loud, whooshing sound and a blast of air that set the bough she was perched on swaying back and forth. When she looked around, she discovered with horror that a large hawk, swooping through the branches, had snapped up a sparrow roosting on the twig above her. It had all happened so quickly that the birds of the Singing Tree could only sit and stare, their mouths still open in mid-song.

Then another, bigger hawk came diving down out of the sky to attack the sparrow hawk. The sparrow hawk, dazed by the unexpected attack, dropped his prize. But just as everyone thought that the little sparrow was saved, the bigger hawk caught him up and flew off back up into the sky.

'Burdock!' cried Bud, bobbing up and down on his branch. A chorus of pleading chirping rose up. But there was nothing any of them could do. The hawk was much too big. When they saw that there was no help for their friend, the birds of the Singing Tree turned back to their morning chorus as if nothing had even happened.

Jenny just clung to her twig in shock. She had been speaking to Burdock only the night before. He had been telling her all about the shenanigans that he and Bud had been up to: stealing the farmer's grain and sipping the cat's milk.

'Frightening, isn't it?' said Peat. 'It could have been any one of us. Poor little Burdock. He was so young. He didn't even get a chance to mate. Well, *que sera, sera*. Life must go on.'

'How can you say that?' Jenny cried, her eyes brimming with tears. 'When one of your friends has just died before your eyes?'

'But these things happen all the time. My cousin was eaten alive by a housecat,' Peat told her, turning his head away, his little beady eyes touched with a tear of great sorrow. 'His life passed before him almost as fast as that scruffy feline's tonsils! Ghastly!' He snatched up a passing ladybug in his beak. 'And my aunt Buttercup, she flew straight into the mouth of one of those guzzlehawks.'

'Guzzlehawks?' asked Jenny.

'Yes, yes, guzzlehawks,' said Peat impatiently. 'Huge, shiny birds that are as big as a house. Bigger. They like to make all that noise, always growling and spluttering. You know, I have never seen one of them ever flap its wings. Now that's technique.'

Suddenly it struck Jenny that Peat was talking about an aeroplane! She laughed, but the sound came out as a high-pitched twitter.

'What's so funny?' scowled Peat. 'My aunt was turned into pillow-stuffing in two seconds flat. That's no laughing matter.'

'Dreadful!' said Jenny.

'And let's see, my great-aunt Bluegrass built her nest on a tractor engine. My sister-in-law was sucked into a heat vent and never seen again. My friend -'

'I think I've heard enough!' Jenny interrupted him. 'What I would like to know is how you manage to enjoy life at all -?'

'You mean all the hunting and escaping? The starvation and suffering, teetering perpetually on the precipice between life and death?' asked Peat.

'Yes,' said Jenny. 'Why do you even bother to get up in the morning at all?'

Peat looked at her before snatching up a passing mayfly.

'The grub's not bad,' he said, munching contentedly away on the unfortunate insect.

A few hours later, the sun was at its highest point in the sky, midday, and it was shrivellingly hot. From her perch in the shelter of the cherry tree, Jenny looked out into the great blue beyond. It hadn't rained for weeks and the ground looked parched and dusty from thirst. The black-eyed susans and the daisies were twitching and blinking in the sun, bending in obeisance to a passing breeze that made the golden wheat of the field ripple like the sea. Jenny bathed in the fleeting coolness of the breeze. But as quickly as it came, it went, and the stillness of the heat was upon them again, like a heavy parka that you couldn't get unzipped.

'It is very warm, isn't it?' Peat shifted from one little leg to the other. He was far too excitable to stay in any one place for too long, even in the heat. He hopped up on a branch, turned around and hopped back again. Then he did it again. If a bird could pace, he was pacing.

'I can't ever remember it being so hot at this time of the year,' said Rosehip, sharpening her beak against the tree trunk.

Jenny was always surprising herself with some new feat of dexterity. Her newest discovery was that she was able to put her head completely through her legs and stare up at the sky between her tail feathers. Now that's something she would never have been able to do as a human. She repeated this trick whenever she would think of it, which was often enough, and quite distracting to the others, to say the least.

'Stop that!' cried Peat, disgusted. 'You have some very peculiar habits.'

'Oh, was I doing it again?' said Jenny, righting herself. 'I just can't get used to being so flexible.'

There was a boy in school, a grade above Jenny, who was double-jointed, or at least that is what she had heard. He was supposed to be able to put both feet completely behind his head and walk on his bottom for an impressive distance, or so, as Toadflax the bard owl would say, legend had it.

'I think we better get some grub,' said Peat.

55

'It's awfully hot, Peat. We might get sunstroke.'

'You're always worrying,' Peat scolded her. 'You think too much. You have to learn not to think, like me. I never think. I just do, do, do. Seize the day. That's what I say. Get on your tap shoes, and we'll make hay.'

They started off into the air. Jenny was a little unsteady, still unused to this new mode of transportation. She felt dizzy as the wind rushed up on her and buffeted her small body. At least it was cooling. Despite everything, the feeling of freedom was like nothing else in the world. To fly like a bird, to leave everything behind, all your troubles, all the people that annoy you - just to fly - was intoxicating. No cares in the world.

Pack up your troubles in your old kit bag, and fly, fly, fly...

They flew over trees and fields and Jenny looked down and saw her neighbour Mrs Macguire in her garden, filling up her fishpond, and Mr Macguire mowing the lawn, his handkerchief knotted around his bald head.

They flew until they came to a newly tilled field, ready for sowing. The farmer was just finishing ploughing the earth with his huge, noisy tractor. Peat told Jenny that this was the best time to come to the field, because all the worms would have been dug up out of the earth and they could have a feast.

In one quick movement, Peat snapped up an earthworm from the freshly turned soil.

'There, 'he said, flopping the worm down in front of her. 'You can have that one.'

Jenny used to pass hours turning over rocks to see what lived in the soggy earth underneath, but she had never had the urge to eat any of the slimy or multi-legged wriggly things she had found there. Perhaps she just hadn't been hungry enough.

'I think you'll find them quite delectable,' said Peat, gulping down another worm. 'And very high in protein. You can't go too far wrong with a worm for breakfast. Or for lunch. It has all the essential nutrients and vitamins that will give you a healthy start for your day.'

'Well, here goes!' Jenny said, grabbing one up gingerly in her little beak and swallowing. The worm floated down her throat, as smooth as silk. It had a wonderful flavour, unlike anything she had ever tasted. Not sweet, but savoury, like a grilled steak and mushrooms, or maybe like a fresh lobster tail, the best part. And ever so juicy.

'They're scrumptious!' she said delightedly, smacking her beak. 'I had no idea. Show me some other good things to eat.'

Peat took her to an old fallen oak tree, covered with fuzzy green moss and rippling wedges of fungi, the kind that Jenny used to collect and etch pictures on with the end of a compass. 'I was saving this for later,' he said solemnly. 'Nobody knows about this place, but I suppose I could share it with you. Try some of this,' he said, nibbling a little of the green moss.

'It is pleasant,' said Jenny. 'Sweet and very refreshing.'

'Well, that's just the appetiser,' said Peat. He

pushed back some of the drooping bark and pulled up a mouthful of squirming pale, white grubs. Jenny surprised herself by gasping in delight.

'Oh, give us some of those,' she said greedily.

'These grubs are the larva of a very rare icunuemen tree wasp. They're a great delicacy. Here, have some of the moss - it really complements the grubs.'

When they had finished their gourmet lunch, they had a drink in the gurgling stream that ran through the forest floor. To Jenny, the forest was like a universe spreading above her. The fluttering leaves of the trees caught the sun like stars. The moss-draped logs crossing the stream, and the ferns and stones were like mountains and primeval trees from some prehistoric landscape. She imagined it was the way the earth would have been at the time of the dinosaurs. And the smells: the sweet smell of the wet forest floor, of mulched leaves, the perfume of cedars and spruce; the bitter tang of trilliums, the red flowers that flourished in the shade of the forest.

They passed a poor dead rabbit. It was being eaten hungrily by maggots. That's interesting, Jenny thought. A rabbit dies, it's eaten by maggots, those maggots are eaten by birds and those birds could be eaten - oh, perish the thought! She shuddered. She would prefer it if the food chain ended at the birds.

Even the forest was like a living creature. It lived and breathed, some part of it always dying and some other being born. One animal dying meant survival for another. For the first time, Jenny realised that, whether she liked it or not, she was a part of this cycle.

Suddenly, the earth seemed to move, throwing Jenny off balance on her stone and nearly tossing her into the water. A great moose appeared out of the woods to take a drink in the stream. It looked as big as a brachiosaur to Jenny. She had never seen one so close. After the moose had drunk its fill, he lifted his big, shaggy head up to stare long and hard at Jenny. He seemed to look straight through her, and she once more felt an uncomfortable thrill up her spine. Then the moose turned and ambled back into the forest.

To get some dessert, Peat took her to an exposed side of a hill, where, to Jenny's amazement, a black bear was contentedly grazing on a crop of wild strawberries.

'What a wonderful, terrifying place this is,' said Jenny.

Chapter Ten

Now Peat and Jenny were flying high above the treetops, above a forest of poplars and maples, their silvery leaves fluttering and sparkling in the sun. They dodged a telegraph pole where a dozen roosting martens cheered as they passed by. They flew past a fuzzy, waving tamerac tree, then down along the channel of an old road and down a hill until they came to a pass where the trees parted to a large lake, fed by a long, winding river. It was Lake Omegod, and the river was the Mactaquac River.

'Oh, I remember this lake,' cried Jenny. 'I used to come here to go swimming when we came here first!'

On the far side of the lake was a small strip of pebbles and grey sand. But the red and white buoys that marked out the beach from the lake were covered with algae. The lifeguard's chair had a broken leg and leaned precariously to one side. It looked as if the little beach hadn't been used for a long time.

'There's something not quite right here, something amiss,' said Peat. 'I can almost smell it.'

It was difficult to avoid smelling it. As soon as

they approached the river, they were overcome with a rotten deathlike stench. It was so strong that they had to take a moment to catch their breath.

Everywhere they looked they could see fish, bloated and discoloured, bobbing on the surface of the lake. A duck floated upside down on the water. When Jenny looked down, she saw a little turtle paddle very slowly, then sink to the lake bottom and be still.

She remembered the lake as alive with the croaking of bullfrogs and the ch-ch-ch-ch of cicada beetles high on the treetops, but now, in the heat of the day, the lake was as quiet as death. The only sound was the buzzing of hungry flies.

'This lake has really gone to the dogs,' said Peat. 'It used to be a wonderful place for a dip, but it's all ruined now. I'll have to tell the council about this at the meeting tomorrow.' Peat caught a drunken-looking dragonfly and spat it out again. 'Oh, that tasted terrible!' he cried. 'Even the local cuisine is off!'

It was as bad as her father had said, and worse. It was the first time Jenny had ever been faced with the disaster of pollution, and she felt sick with shame. More than anything, she wanted to be on one of her father's nature trips, listening to one of his talks on ecology. She wanted to do something.

They glided over the lake, watching their reflections on the glinting surface of the water below. It swirled in a hundred colours, colours that Jenny had never seen in water before. At first the water seemed green, then it looked blue, then purple, and red, and then green again.

But as they flew, there was one more reflection that Jenny didn't see. A large, black reflection, coming up on their tail.

'Watch out!' Peat cried. 'Behind you, Jenny. Behind!'

Jenny flew as fast as her little wings could carry her, but no matter how fast she went, the ugly, black bird above her was stronger and bigger and came up swiftly behind her. She could see his huge, curved, white beak, a beak designed for ripping and tearing the flesh of little birds, and his big, thick talons, each nail long enough to make a robin into a shish kebab.

'Come over here, you big ugly galoot. You old piece of fish bait!'

Peat was doing an admirable job of trying to distract the crow, but one flick of its tattered black wing sent Peat flying. He just managed to catch himself before he landed in the lake's stinking waters.

'It's you I desire, my pretty,' hissed the crow, his low, gravelly voice just above her. Jenny could see one of his beady black eyes blinking. 'Come into my gullet, said the spider to the fly.'

Where had she heard that voice before? Jenny was exhausted. She didn't think she could fly a flap further. This must be it, thought Jenny. She was going to fill in her part of the food chain.

The crow was almost on her, his curling toes reaching out to grab her. And then he had her!

She felt his sharp claws stabbing into her little body and the rush of pain and terror overwhelmed her. But then there was a terrible jolt and Jenny felt herself being hurled through the air upside down, and then landing with an awful crash in a prickly raspberry bush.

'Jenny, are you all right?' asked Peat, flying quickly to her side. 'You didn't break anything?'

'Oh! Not again!' she cried, pulling a raspberry thorn from her toe. 'Ouch! Am I still alive?' Her heart was beating so hard she thought it would burst out of her chest. Suddenly she felt like crying.

'If it hurts, you are,' said Peat, breathlessly. 'I can't believe you got away. That crow was really set on catching you. I've never seen any crow so eager. They're not hunting birds. They usually eat what's left over from another animal. They almost never kill on their own.'

'How did I get away?' Jenny panted. 'I felt his claws digging in me!'

Peat nodded to a sign, and they hopped over to it. DANGER! NO SWIMMING. POLLUTED WATERS. The crow had crashed headlong into it, and was now lying in a crumpled heap.

Where had she seen it before? The grey plumage around its back, like a grey vest, was familiar. It wasn't a bird common to this area, that was for sure.

'I think we better hit the road,' said Peat. 'I don't want to be around when he wakes up.'

Chapter Eleven

'Behold the egg,' said Professor Wren, presenting his family with his boiled egg and twirling it in the bright white light of morning for all to see and admire. 'Nature's greatest mystery. All the secrets of life, the universe, and everything bundled up into in a little, wee shell.'

'Leo, eat your egg before it gets cold,' said Mrs Wren, plopping the rest of the eggs into egg cups shaped like miniature glass chickens and distributing them around the table.

'Life, death, and renewal is the egg. A source of life for us, a source of death for the foetal chicken –'

'Oh, Dad, you're going to make me sick!' cried Alice.

'– and a symbol of life everlasting: the seed, the nut, the packaging of brand-new life born out of the old.'

'Which came first, the chicken or the egg?' said Henry, proud of his deep, philosophical contribution to the breakfast table.

'Which, indeed! It questions the very origins of life itself. I would like to make a toast,' said Professor Wren, and all the family humoured him by raising their egg cups. 'To the humble egg. Its mystery lives on in each new dozen, and that's no yolk! Keep your eggs up! That's not the only toast. This morning I got a letter from the World Wildlife Trust, and they have selected me, Leo Wren, research scientist extraordinaire, to accept a donation cheque on their behalf from the esteemed company, Acid Drops & Lollipops, Inc., in recognition of my humble efforts to preserve the wildlife of this country. Cin cin!'

'Cin, cin!' the rest of the family said, clicking their eggs together.

'But that's not all,' said Professor Wren. 'This presentation is going to be on national television, so I am going to take the opportunity of making a contribution of my own.'

'That's what I was afraid of,' said Mrs Wren, sighing as she sat down and took a weary bite of her toast.

'There has been suspicions that nuclear waste is being shipped into this country and buried somewhere in this province. I am going to raise an appeal for information. I think the public have a right to know what is happening to their land.'

'But Leo, you don't have any proof.'

'I have photographs. I know this truck is involved. And I'm certain that's why my lab was turned upside down. Someone was looking for something very specific.'

'It sounds very dangerous, Dad,' said Henry. 'What if the people who are doing the polluting don't like what you're doing?'

'It's a chance I have to take. This opportunity is to good to pass up. And they can't avoid listening to me on national television.'

'But what about all that equipment?' asked Mrs Wren. 'Can you have it replaced?'

'No, but it doesn't matter. I won't be needing half that equipment anyway.' Professor Wren sipped his tea thoughtfully. 'I think I'm coming to a dead end with my research. I haven't made any discoveries on the language of birds for a year. I don't think I'll be getting my grant renewed this year, I'm sure of it. I may be a very good environmentalist, but I'm a very bad scientist.'

'That's not true,' said Mrs Wren.

'Besides, now Louis has gone, too. I think someone is trying to tell me something.'

'Louis has gone?' Jenny's mother asked, one hand trying to prevent 'Jenny' from eating off her plate, the other trying to pick up her cup of instant coffee.

'Yes,' said Professor Wren. 'He just came to me and thanked me for everything, said I had a lovely family, and wished me prosperity throughout this life and the other ones to come. Then he left.'

'Just like that?' said Mrs Wren.

'Just like that,' said Professor Wren.

'Weird,' said Henry.

'I'll miss him,' said Mrs Wren. 'Maybe it was my imagination, but he just made everything around him brighter. Now, come on, Jenny, eat your egg. You want to grow up to be big and strong, don't you?'

'You can't make me eat it!' her daughter cried

66

and pushed herself from the table so violently that everyone's eggs fell out of their cups and went rolling away along the table.

'Jenny', as you might have guessed, was not herself this morning. The truth of the matter was that Jenny was Twill, the robin. When Jenny had taken Twill's body, Twill had taken hers. They had changed places!

'OK, OK,' said Jenny's mother. 'You don't have to eat your egg. Have some cereal instead,' and she filled up a bowl with cornflakes. Twill liked this much better, clumsily grabbing fistfuls of flakes and stuffing them into her mouth before Mrs Wren got a chance to pour on the milk.

'Jenny!' said Mrs Wren. 'Use a spoon, please.'

Twill took the spoon Mrs Wren gave her. She was just getting used to having hands and being able to pick things up. It seemed a very complicated affair, this eating. First she had to pick up the food from a dish with this metal object and then direct it to this hole in her head which was her mouth. It was more difficult than she thought. What she did manage to get on her spoon ended up over her shoulder or on her lap. She didn't understand what all the fuss was about, anyway. The food wasn't going anywhere. It must be long dead, Twill thought. She preferred the thrill of the chase. At least you could be sure your food was fresh.

'That company,' said Mrs Wren, starting to clear away the breakfast dishes. 'Acid Drops & Lollipops. Their factory is up on Kenwick's Mountain, isn't it? I always thought it was a bit strange, a sweet factory hidden deep in God's armpit, way up there in the mountains. And they don't employ any local people, only people from foreign countries. I met a few of them in the supermarket and they can't even speak English.'

'Listen,' said Professor Wren, helping himself to another boiled egg. 'Any company that donates a cheque for fifteen thousand dollars to the WWF can't be such a bad lot, especially with a name like Acid Drops & Lollipops Incorporated. Have you ever incorporated any of their sweets, Maura? Darn fine candies they are, too.'

'Look,' Mrs Wren said. 'A robin sitting on the window ledge. They certainly seem to be getting very brazen these days.' She looked over at the little bird peering in through the latticed windows. 'Go and throw a crust to it, Alice.'

Twill was fascinated with all the things on the table and curious as to what they tasted like. She now had a tongue that she could stick out of her mouth, and she was busily licking everything on the table. Most things didn't taste like much, but there were smooth things and rough things, and warm things and cool things. Twill tasted a cold glass of orange juice and then a very hot teapot.

'Ow!' she cried.

'Jenny certainly seems to be behaving oddly,' remarked her father as Twill squeezed her injured tongue.

'Yes, Leo,' said Mrs Wren. 'Last night, she slept the whole night perched on the back of her chair, with her head under her arm. And her loud singing at dawn! I'm worried she's going to do something very strange. Maybe we'd better call the doctor. It might be some rare virus.'

'Still hungry,' cried Twill. 'Any worms or beetles?'

'Oh, it's only one of those pubescent phases she's going through,' said Professor Wren, unfolding his newspaper and starting to read. 'I'm sure she'll snap out of it.'

Chapter Twelve

The Birds' Council was a very solemn affair and took place on a large oak tree on the edge of the forest. The elders sat perched on a large thick branch. The head of the assembly was a cardinal, an impressive, red-crested bird whom everyone knew as Cardinal Redcap. Four elder birds made up the council, two bluejays and a yellow grosbeak and a little green finch called Meadowsweet who acted as presenter.

'Ahem! Ahem!' Cardinal Redcap cleared his throat loudly and waited for the onlooking crowd to settle down. 'First item for discussion on the Spring Season.'

Meadowsweet, the presenter, hopped forward on the bough. 'Um. First item, ahh. The Weather.'

After a few minutes, a tiny spotted flycatcher hopped meekly forward.

'Speak, bird, speak.' The cardinal ruffled his feathers impatiently.

'Your honour, your gracious, I have reason to think there will be a drought this summer!'

Echoes of 'Drought, drought!' could be heard throughout the crowd.

'And what proof do you have of this?' asked the cardinal.

'I had a dream,' said the flycatcher. 'In my dream, there were seven bushes with ripe raspberries on them. Then seven more bushes grew up, right there on the spot, and uprooted those bushes. Then another bush came along and ate those bushes. Then the bushes that were left withered and died so that there wasn't one left.'

'A sure sign that there will be a drought this year!' Cardinal Redcap cried. 'So listen to me, citizens! We can't allow any more newcomers to the area. They will all have to go to another district. We have to look after our food supplies.'

'He knows there is going to be a drought from that flycatcher's dream?' Jenny whispered.

'Yes,' said Peat. 'Lots of things get decided on by dreams and visions.'

'Silence! Silence!' Cardinal Redcap ordered. 'Item Two.'

'Ahh,' said Peat, hopping forward nervously. 'I have an item. Yesterday, myself and our new friend, Jenny, went to visit Lake Omegod. It was in a horrible state. It was polluted, fouled, defiled. There were dead animals floating in it. I tasted an insect and had to spit it out!'

'He spat it out!' the crowd cried. If Peat wouldn't eat it, it must have been inedible.

'There are dark forces at work here,' said Cardinal Redcap. 'First it was Otter's Pond, and now Lake Omegod. Look, members. First there is drought and now plague! The end of the world is nigh!'

'The end of the world is coming! The end of the world is coming!' It was clear that all the birds in the tree were enjoying the evening's drama. No wonder they all flocked from near and far to see it. And the cardinal knew how to put on a good show.

'Wait! I think I know who might be responsible,' piped up Jenny, pushing her way though the crowd to stand before the cardinal. 'A candy factory in the mountains called Acid Drops & Lollipops.'

Everybody gasped. Jenny looked from bird to bird, trying to figure out what she could have said to cause their shocked expressions.

'This is blasphemy!' Cardinal Redcap flourished his wings dramatically to the crowd. 'The woe that this wretched newcomer brings upon us! We have a heathen in our midst!'

'A heathen?' said Jenny in bewilderment.

Peat sidled up to his friend in an effort to put her right. 'You said the name that our sacred religion decrees must never pass our beaks,' he whispered. 'It means everything horrible and awful in the world. It's evil! It's a name for a desperate place deep in the darkest pit under the great mountain, and those who go there are never seen again.'

'Oh, wow!' said Jenny. 'Do you know how to get there?'

'To get there!' Peat looked at his friend with dismay. 'Why would anyone want to get there?'

'We might be able to stop it!'

'Stop the demon! Stop the plague!' thundered Cardinal Redcap in a loud, mocking tone. 'This little robin is going to tell us how to end the catastrophe!'

'How do we stop it?' asked one of the elder jays, showing more interest than Cardinal Redcap would have liked.

Jenny bravely addressed the president, the elders and the whole flock of birds in the old oak tree. 'Unless you want to give up your lake, we have to do something about it! We will have to go to this place, find out what they're doing, and then stop it!'

'And get burned to a crisp by the fiery breath of devils,' said Cardinal Redcap. 'I don't think so!'

Then suddenly the whole tree shook and a great grey owl flew in amongst the birds, sending many birds falling off their perch, so great was his size and power. He landed on the branch of the elders, throwing the two jays and the cardinal off their perch of honour.

'It's Old Hornbeam,' cried the crowd. 'Hornbeam! Hornbeam!' Jenny could hear the birds whispering amongst themselves. Most of them would never have seen Old Hornbeam. He was just like a legend, a god who lived at the top of the tree.

'I believe,' the old owl began slowly, 'that what this robin called Jenny says is true. I have lived many, many years and have seen the slow destruction of our land by man. We must do something about it.'

'But, sir, Mr Hornbeam, lord, sir,' dithered Cardinal Redcap, 'the demon lives in the place she named. We were told...'

Old Hornbeam opened his great speckled

wings and flapped them mightily, so that all the party held on for dear life to their branches against the heat. 'Don't tell me about your stupid superstitions!' he bellowed angrily. Every bird on the tree trembled with fright. 'If I had my way I would eat the whole Council for breakfast. I have listened to all your didgery-dooing. Rule this and rule that. We have to do something about this, or it will be the end of the world for us! A time will come when we will have no food to eat, and nothing to drink. Then what will you do?'

Cardinal Redcap had no answer. The assembly stared in stunned silence.

Having said his piece, Old Hornbeam left the council meeting. It would be the last time that any of the birds on the tree would see him. He flew back to his perch on top of the Singing Tree and, for all I know, he's there still.

Back at the cherry tree, the birds discussed the events of the evening. Jenny was more determined than ever to go and find out what this factory was up to, and to try to put a stop to it. She made a plan to go to Kenwick Mountain the very next day.

'But what can we do?' Peat asked. 'We'll come with you, but we've no power in the human world.'

Jenny thought for a moment. An idea came to her. She had a little power in the human world, or at least she used to have. She would ask a friend to help her.

Later that evening, they were visited at the Singing Tree by an unusual flock of foreign visitors.

'Where are we?' asked one of the storks in a peculiar accent. 'I don't recognise dis place at all. I think we were steered off course. Ees dis Spain?'

'No,' said Rosehip, squinting down at them in disbelief from her perch. 'You're in Canada.'

'Canada! Dis is all your fault!' one stork hollered at another, giving him an almighty clout that sent him reeling backwards.

'I didn't know,' said the clouted stork, who must have been the navigator for this trip. 'I was sure I was going in the right direction. I can't think what went wrong.'

'You went wrong, beetlebrain!' said another stork, belting him with his wing, sending him swaying. 'What did you think you were doing following dose ships, you puddlehead? Now what are we going to do?'

'I don't think you can stay here,' said Rosehip. 'The council said we couldn't allow any more immigrants.'

'You're welcome,' said Toadflax to the storks, ignoring Rosehip. 'The council can go take a flying leap.'

'What will you have to eat?' asked Rosehip politely. 'You must be very hungry after your trip.'

'Do you have any fresh Chaldean locusts?' asked one stork.

'No, I don't think so,' answered Rosehip after a

little thought.

'How about some Moroccan grasshoppers?'

'How about some bugs and worms?' offered Rosehip.

'Bugs and worms?' said the first stork in indignation. 'How disgusting! Are you sure you don't have any African elephant locusts?'

There was great chatter and merriment at the Singing Tree that evening. Many of the birds who had come from other parts of the forest for the council meeting stayed on, and they were squeezed together like so many sardines in a can. And the singing, Jenny was sure, could be heard from miles around. They also swopped stories and jokes. The storks captivated the residents with their feather-raising tales of their adventures in exotic lands, while Olio and Bruno serenaded them with arias from Italian aviaries.

'How many South African willow warblers does it take to catch a glow-worm?' asked one of the storks. No one knew. 'Twenty-five!' the stork crowed with laughter. 'One to pick up the glow worm off da branch and twenty-four to help him! Ha!'

Everyone groaned. They were getting quite tired of willow warbler jokes.

'*Volare!* Tweet-tweet-tweet. *Cantare!* Tweet-tweet-tweet-tweet!' Bruno and Olio trilled with great energy into the soft evening air. 'Oh, sol-lay meeeo ...'

'Isn't this wonderful, Jenny?' chirped Peat, swaying to the music. 'I always look forward to our friends visiting us from overseas, but this is an unexpected treat!'

But Jenny was confused. How could they be so happy when Hornbeam had predicted doom for the planet?

'If we didn't enjoy ourselves, our life would be meaningless. Every day would bring unhappiness and heartbreak,' said Toadflax wisely. 'Our lives are short and so fragile. We must make merry while we can.'

Jenny tried to enjoy the evening, but she felt very uneasy. She felt as though someone or something was watching her. Perched on a telephone pole across the garden was a large, black bird. It was the same crow that had attacked her at Lake Omegod, and it was staring directly at her. She couldn't move. She was pinned by the crow's stare.

Then suddenly a great golden bird came swooping from the sky and attacked the crow, throwing it off its perch. They wrestled until the crow escaped and flew unsteadily into the shelter of the trees.

Chapter Thirteen

Jenny landed on the windowsill. She peered into the glass but saw no one, and the emptiness of the house made her feel lonely for her family.

She could see across the dinner table and into the living room. That's funny, she thought to herself. The television was on. She could see what looked like the news, and though she couldn't hear what was being said, she recognised straight away the rumpled, pin-striped suit of her father.

What was he doing on television?

Jenny scanned the garden and when she could find neither sight nor sound of any of her family, she decided to check in the laboratory. She wanted to find Louis. More than anyone, Louis would understand.

The door of the lab was open and she fluttered in. But the moment she entered, the door shut with an awful bang behind her! Inside, everything was quiet except for the usual hubbub of the birds.

'Oh, look who's here,' cried a speckled nutcracker.

'Well, la de da, isn't it Twill the robin out for a preamble? Coming to pay your poor fellow inmates a visit, for old times' sake?' another bird jeered.

'Louis, Louis, Louis!' she called, but she got no answer.

'You know we never really liked you, in case you didn't know,' another bird cawed. 'You were always such a know-all, and a pet.'

Now she understood what Twill had been talking about. These birds were bullies.

Jenny wondered where Louis could have got to. Could he have gone into the city with her father? She doubted that he would leave the lab unattended.

But then, as she looked around, her heart nearly stopped. There, clutching the edge of the linoleum-topped table with its huge, thorny feet, was the crow! The bird that had haunted her like an unwanted shadow, lurking and waiting for her! Now, there it sat, as silent as death, watching her.

And now it truly had her at its mercy. She was trapped in the laboratory. The screen door had shut behind her. There was nowhere to go.

'W-who are you?' she stuttered. 'What do you want?'

'Remember I came to visit you?' said the crow in a sweet voice. 'Your father had something I wanted and then I cut myself on something here in this very lab, and now I'm a changeling, just like you.'

'You're Professor Mennis!' Jenny cried, frozen with terror. 'What do you want with me?'

The bird leaned towards her, blinking and

clacking its nasty beak. 'You're a pest, Jenny Wren, and you know too much. I'm afraid I'll have to dispose of you.'

There was a loud, tinny ring-ring of a bicycle bell, and then Blake came bursting through the door.

'Jenny! Jenny, are you in here?' he called her. Blake looked around the laboratory, but could see no sign of Jenny anywhere. All he saw were two birds staring up at him. A robin and a very rough-looking crow.

'You must have got out of your cages,' said Blake. 'I'll have to tell Professor Wren.'

'Help me, Blake,' Jenny cried, flying over to land on the microscope in front of him. 'I'm right here!'

Blake frowned. He could hear Jenny's voice and he decided it must be coming from outside the laboratory. He pushed back through the screen door and Jenny decided she would make a run for it. She just managed to get through, feeling the door pinch one of her tail feathers as it slammed closed. But she was through! The crow, who must have followed her, wasn't so lucky and he crashed straight into the door. 'Whew!' said Jenny. 'That was close.'

'Jenny! Where are you?' Blake called again, sheltering his eyes from the bright sun.

Jenny hopped on to the roof of one of the bird feeders in front of him. This one was in the shape of a two-storey beige bungalow, complete with patio and sun umbrella. 'I'm here, Blake! In front of you!' she chirped as loudly as she could.

Blake looked around but could see no one. Jenny hopped from the bird bungalow on to his shoulder and he drew back with surprise. 'Now can you see me?' she piped into his ear.

'Ow! Yes! Jenny, is that you?' Blake asked, his eyes widening in disbelief.

'Yes, you blubberhead, it's me! What do you think?'

'But you're a bird!' Blake exclaimed, scratching his head in puzzlement. 'I mean, why, or how, did it happen?' He was so shocked that he had to sit down on the lawn. Jenny hopped from his shoulder to rest on the toe of his sneaker, from which she watched him earnestly.

'I don't know,' she said. 'I don't know or understand what happened to me, but there are more serious things to discuss. I can't find Louis, so I guess you'll have to do.'

'Well, since you put it that way -' began Blake, but Jenny interrupted.

'I need your help, Blake. The Acid Drops & Lollipops factory is up to some stuff. Somehow they're polluting Lake Omegod. You have to come. Tonight.'

'Acid Drops & Lollipops?' repeated Blake, trying to concentrate on what the little bird on his sneaker was trying to tell him. It was no easy task. 'Isn't it that place that makes the Cosmic candy bar?'

'That's the one!'

'I don't know,' said Blake. 'It's a long way away. I was going to visit Chris Johnson. We were going to go swimming. That's why I came over.'

'I hope you're not thinking of going to Lake Omegod. You might never come out. The lake is polluted. There's a sign up and everything.'

'Oh well, we could always go somewhere else.'

'Don't you want to put all those nature walks to some use?' said Jenny, hopping on to his arm and peering intently up at him. 'All that stuff my father was teaching you about the environment. Don't you want to do something about it?'

'I only joined the scouts because of -' Blake broke off quickly.

'Because of what?' asked Jenny, staring at him with one of her black, unblinking eyes.

'It doesn't matter,' said Blake, irritated with himself. 'OK. I'll go. But you're not going to do anything crazy, are you?'

'Crazy? Me?' Jenny was shocked. 'Look at me. I'm a bird. How much crazier can I get?' She beat her wings and rose up into the air, just to demonstrate. She never thought of herself as someone who did crazy things. She always thought she was boring. Everyone in her family seemed more exciting than her.

'That's nothing for you,' said Blake. 'Do you remember the time a couple of years ago, when you first came, when we went skating on the river? You got some crazy idea to bring one of your mother's blankets and make a sail. Then a wind blew up and we were blown nearly all the way to Saint John on the river. We had to borrow money from your cousin who worked at the bank to buy a ticket home again. I was grounded for nearly a month over that.'

'It was an experiment,' said Jenny defensively. 'How did I know it was going to work so well?'

'And how about last year, that time when we went to the beach?' said Blake, clearly enjoying his opportunity to prove a point. 'You made a sailboat out of a big styrofoam block. The styrofoam was so light and the current so strong, it didn't matter which way you turned the sail, we just went in the one direction, and very fast too! We nearly sailed all the way to Saint John, and we had to -'

'Yes, I know,' said Jenny, 'we had to borrow more money from my cousin who worked in the bank to buy a ticket and take the train home.'

'I was grounded for two months over that. I couldn't even swim then!' said Blake.

Jenny was pleased by his account of her shenanigans. She had nearly forgotten them. 'Well, are you going to do it or what?' she demanded.

'I suppose I don't have any choice, do I?' said Blake, smiling. 'I must admit that breaking into a candy factory has its attractive points.'

Suddenly they heard cries and shouting coming from the rear of the house. Blake ran to see what was the matter, and Jenny flew behind him ...

Chapter Fourteen

Jenny recognised her mother's voice. 'Jenny, don't do it! Please, come down!'

'Jenny, why are you always trying to embarrass us? Everybody is going to think we're a bunch of lunatics!' Alice's voice.

Jenny flew over to the rear of the house and came to rest on a garden gnome perched amongst a clump of lupins. Her mother and sister were looking up to the roof where she saw her very own body crouched. Her body was glancing nervously this way and that, flapping its arms as if they were wings.

Oh, that's just terrific, Jenny thought to herself. By the time I get back to my own body, it will be in a cast. That's just what I need!

'I want out!' cried the 'Jenny' on the roof. 'I feel trapped. I want to fly. I want to be free, iddle-iddle-eep!'

Jenny watched herself teetering dangerously on the edge of the roof, flapping her arms like a fool. She decided that she wasn't just going to sit there and watch her body break into a hundred pieces. She had to do something about it. She flew up to the rooftop.

'Is that you, Twill, you dope?' Jenny said,

landing on her own knee. 'It's me, Jenny.'

'Oh, Jenny! You look, look just like me! Tweet!'

'We've changed places, you twit! I don't know how it happened but it has. So get down off this roof this moment. I want something left of my body when I change back.'

'Do you think we will, Jenny?' asked Twill with tears in 'her' eyes. 'I hate being you. Nobody pays any attention to me. I feel invisible, unwanted, unloved.'

'That sounds just about right,' said Jenny.

'No, Jenny!' her mother shouted from below. 'Stay where you are! Don't move!'

'I want to be a bird again. I want to be a robin!' whimpered Twill.

'How did you get up here, anyway?' said Jenny, hopping on top of the chimney and peering into its blackness.

Twill pointed down to Jenny's bedroom window. 'From there.'

'Well, however you got up, get down!' said Jenny, not bothering to look where Twill was pointing.

Without another word, Twill turned on her belly and began lowering herself over the roof edge until she was hanging on only by her fingers.

'Is that how you got up?' Jenny squeaked in horror, hopping on to the gutter. 'Are you crazy? Do you want to get me killed?'

'All the saints in heaven.' Mrs Wren closed her eyes in silent prayer. 'Please, save my daughter. I promise to be a better mother!'

But with one rapid, agile movement, Twill swung herself feet first into Jenny's open window. The next moment, Jenny was watching Twill munching from a package of sesame seeds. Jenny hopped on to her window ledge.

'Wasn't that just the coolest thing you've ever seen?' said Blake as Jenny emerged a minute later from the house with Twill behind, still gorging herself on sesame seeds. Mrs Wren clasped her.

'You won't say anything about this to anyone?' Alice whispered to Blake. 'I don't think I could stand the embarrassment. One more thing like this and the men in the white coats will be on our doorstep.'

'What are you going to do to persuade me?' said Blake, puckering his mouth in a kiss.

'I'd rather die, you little twerp!' sneered Alice and walked back into the house.

'Oh, Jenny,' Mrs Wren cried, 'don't ever do anything bird-brained like that again. It's all my fault. I've been a lousy mother. I promise I'm going to try harder.' She hugged and squeezed Twill, making her cough up her sesame seeds. 'Let me look at you.' Mrs Wren straightened Twill's hair. 'I should have known you were unhappy, but I have been so busy. I always believed in the theory of non-interactive parenting, but I should have known it wouldn't work on all my children. I'm never going to neglect you again.'

Blake walked over to Jenny, perched again on the garden gnome and sharpening her beak on its nose. 'I think your sister will come around in time,' he said, smirking.

'Do you have any idea how humiliating this is?' Jenny cried. 'Look at my body! It almost committed suicide on my behalf. My body is behaving like a moron and everyone thinks it's me!'

'Blake!' called Jenny's mother, walking over and leading Twill by the hand. 'Would you look after Jenny for a while? I'll pay you!' There was a tinge of desperation in her voice that was hard to ignore.

'No problem, Mrs Wren. I'll look after her. You don't have to pay.'

'Oh, bless you, child,' Mrs Wren cried, rushing into the house.

'Blake, no, don't do it!' piped Jenny, bouncing up and down on the gnome's nose. 'We can't take her with us. She'll spoil everything.'

'I hear you! I hear you!' cried Twill gleefully, scratching her armpit. 'Take me where?'

'I don't think we have much choice,' said Blake. 'I promised your mother I'd look after you, er, Twill. I don't think she'll cause too much trouble.'

'You don't know Twill,' said Jenny, sighing in defeat.

Chapter Fifteen

'Jenny, get out of there!'

Blake yanked at Twill's shirt, trying with all his strength to pull Twill's head, or Jenny's head, out of a foxhole. All the birds grabbed on to Blake as he pulled.

'Heave!' cried Peat. 'Heave!'

'I just hope you haven't broken anything of mine!' said Jenny severely once Twill, her face black with dirt, had been pulled out of the hole. 'Or been putting stuff in my mouth that I wouldn't put there.'

'This is definitely one of your crazy ideas,' said Blake as they scrambled up the steep edge of the gorge, following one of the lumberjack trails. The trails were old, probably hadn't seen one of those lumberjacks of the red plaid coat and brown boot variety for years. Jenny had loved exploring them. They were like giant mazes, and very dangerous. One could easily get lost down these trails.

'I'm sure it's this way,' said Bud, scratching his head with his foot from his perch on a tree stump. 'I'm just not sure what direction.'

'Oh, that's fine, fine, fine,' said Rosehip crossly. 'Why don't we just draw straws and be done with it, it, it?'

'I still don't think we should go,' said Speedwell, the swallow. 'I mean, this is a dangerous place.'

'Do you have any idea where this factory is?' Jenny asked Blake, landing on his shoulder. When he said he didn't, she looked ahead into the deep woods, as if the forest itself could give her some sign - and then it did!

They heard a snapping of twigs and a raccoon plodded out on to the trail ahead of them. The raccoon seemed to take a great interest in them, contemplating them with its bright, intelligent eyes through its bandit's mask. It trundled along the path a little more and then stopped and sat up on its hind legs again, looking at them, its whiskers twitching. It curved one of its long human-like fingers towards them, beckoning to them.

It was Twill who decided to follow it, hopping along on her hunkers behind it. 'We have to follow the raccoon,' she trilled.

'Oh no,' said Blake in alarm. 'Come back, come back.'

'No, wait,' said Jenny. 'Maybe he wants us to follow him. Look, he almost seems to be calling us.'

'Yes, I think that's it!' said Rosehip, shaking her head in frustration. 'Why not follow a raccoon? We've followed Bud.' Bud gave Rosehip a sharp peck.

So they followed the raccoon up the long, winding path. Whenever it seemed as if they were falling behind, the raccoon slowed down and waited for them, his whiskers twitching impatiently.

They passed over a narrow part of the trail and Jenny could hear a rushing stream flowing underneath the path. Ahead of her, barely distinguishable from the ferns, were the remains of an old log cabin.

'I wonder who lived in there?' Blake asked, pushing his way through the bushes to have a closer look.

'Legend has it,' Toadflax began, coming to land on one of its moss-covered logs, 'that an old hermit lived here and used to hunt and live off the land, leaving bits of fat out for the birds and animals in the winter. Some say he died of starvation one very bad winter, but others think he turned into a silver wolf, because his body was never found and a silver wolf can be seen prowling around this house every Winter Solstice. We have always called this part of the woods Hermit's Pass, though the council insists on calling it District 3b.'

Toadflax showed them many other interesting places. Dove's Roost, a huge ash tree where morning doves met every springtime to raise their young. Rabbit's Run, a cluster of pine and cedar trees where nothing would grow because of the high acidity of their dropping needles, which was the favourite haunt of rabbits.

They came to a ridge of granite where flowers were growing straight out of the rockface.

'Legend has it that the great Glooscap passed

over this ridge, leaving the impression of his feet in the rock. Ever since, these flowers have grown right out of the stone!' said Toadflax.

'Who is Glooscap?' asked Jenny.

'Glooscap is a great human god. Legend has it that it was he who turned the hermit into a wolf.'

'Some even say that Old Hornbeam used to be a man who asked Glooscap to make him very wise,' said Rosehip, leaping on to the craggy crest of rock and taking a sip of the stream that ran by it.

The sun was starting to drift eastwards and they came to rest on a collection of poplar trees. Toadflax caught a shrew and ate it in one gulp. Jenny, Peat, Bud and Rosehip looked for grubs for their dinner.

'How can you eat that? That's disgusting!' said Blake, resting on a stone. He was holding Jenny on one hand, feeding her bits of his peanut butter and jelly sandwich.

The raccoon stopped cleaning his whiskers impatiently and waddled off the trail, and back into the woods.

'Well, there goes our guide,' said Rosehip. 'I hope we can find our way without him.'

Suddenly they heard noises: a clacking and banging and a rumble of motor engines. They took to the trail again.

Chapter Sixteen

A huge, monster of a factory loomed before them. A monstrosity of steel and concrete, it clattered and clanged, grunted and groaned, puffing and choking smoke and steam from three grey smokestacks like huge cigars in the sky. There was nothing nice you could say about it. It was noisy and dirty and ... noisy and dirty. It was also very, very big. One could hardly see it all at once. It sprawled as big as a shopping mall and twice as ugly.

A big, glowing sign rose up gaudily in front of them. In curly, neon pink letters was the name. ACID DROPS & LOLLIPOPS, INC.

'And the gates loomed before them like the entrance to the Underworld, a gateway through which all must pass,' said Toadflax grandly.

'Look at it,' gasped Bud. 'Only giants could live in there!'

'We've seen it, now let's go!' said Peat, not wanting to stick around.

'Look!' said Rosehip, indicating a steel wall. At its base were the limp bodies of two swallows.

The other birds gasped and turned away.

'Foreigners,' said Peat, looking down at the crumpled bodies. 'Didn't know about this place, and never heard the council's warnings - look.'

There were other bodies lying around the factory. They counted six dead birds in all.

'A brother of mine is alone and dead in a foreign land. It is sooo sad,' said Olio. 'I think I will sing him a death lament.' He cradled his dead compatriot in his wings.

'The factory didn't kill your countryman,' said Jenny. 'It's whoever is inside that's doing it.'

Their conversation was interrupted by the rumbling from a convoy of transport trucks coming up the lumberjack trail into the factory parking lot. Well, they must be delivering stuff, Jenny thought, why would they need stuff with a skull and crossbones on it to make candies and after-dinner mints? It must be some deadly good new filling, she thought to herself, or maybe not. There was definitely more here than met the eye. 'We have to go in,' she announced simply. She didn't see this as a matter to be quibbled with.

'Are you crazy?' cried Peat. 'Are you mad, totally off your rocker, a few short of a dozen? You can't go in. The giants will eat you alive.'

'What if we get caught?' said Blake.

'We have to take the chance,' said Jenny. 'We all have a duty. We have to find out what is going on here.'

'But Jenny,' squeaked Rosehip, 'we might never come out!'

They watched as one of the drivers got out of his cab to enter the factory through the glass double doors. He took a card that looked like a bank card out of his pocket and stuck it in a little slot beside the door. They could hear a beep and then he opened the door.

'You have to have one of those cards to get in,' said Blake. 'How are we going to do it?'

'This is how,' said Jenny.

The second driver was greedily eating a large submarine sandwich. They watched him finish the sandwich, throw the paper bag over his shoulder and begin walking towards the double door.

'Here. Give me your badge,' Jenny asked Blake.

Blake took off his World Wildlife Trust badge and handed it to Jenny, who took it up in her beak.

'I want to go in!' blurted Twill loudly enough for anyone to hear.

'Shhh!' hissed Blake, clamping her mouth. 'Do you want to get us caught?'

The second truck driver had stopped in his tracks and was looking around to see where the noise had come from. Then, apparently satisfied that it wasn't worth investigating, he rummaged through his back pocket and took out his card.

At that point, Jenny, the badge in her beak, flew down towards the door. When the driver opened the door, Jenny flew down immediately after him and stuck the badge between the door and the jamb, wedging it open.

'Come on,' said Blake. 'Let's go.'

Inside, the factory was dazzlingly bright with stainless steel and alive with all sorts of unnatural-looking machines making all sorts of unnatural noises and doing very unnatural things. There were machines for pumping, and spraying, for folding and flattening. Machines for inflating, machines for deflating. If you went into one of them you could come out nearly any shape you wanted. It was quite frightening to see all that was involved in making harmless little candies that you popped in your mouth and finished in moments.

'I don't see anything,' Blake whispered to Jenny. 'It just looks like a factory to me.'

'How do you know?' she tweeped. 'Do you usually visit factories for fun?'

'No,' said Blake. 'But -'

Before he could even finish, there was a great grumbling and the floor began to shift underneath their feet. Blake, Twill and Jenny and her bird friends had to hold on for dear life as it began to split from the centre, machines and all. Blake and Twill found themselves separating slowly from their friends on the opposite side of the splitting floor. Below them they saw a dark, bottomless pit from which a foul smelling gas poured.

'Blake!' cried Jenny to her friend on the opposite side of the pit. But there was nothing she could do. The exit was on her side. Blake and Twill were trapped.

The ceiling had also parted, and now the sky beamed through clear and blue, blissfully ignorant of the damage it was about to witness. They watched as a crane moved into position, lowering a massive, barrel-shaped container down into the factory. It kept on lowering it until it passed before Jenny's nose and then sank down into the black pit in the floor.

The floor and the ceiling began slowly to close.

Blake and Twill had been watching this spectacle so intently that they hadn't noticed one of the factory guards waving at them excitedly from the other side of the pit.

'Hey, you kids!' he roared through his gas mask. 'What are you doing over here? This is restricted property!'

'We have to get out of here!' cried Blake. But the floor wasn't closing quickly enough and another guard was running down the factory floor, straight for him.

'Hey you,' the other guard called. 'Wait till I get my hands on you!'

'Come on! Close, close!' cried Blake to the slowly closing floor. The guard was nearly at them. 'We'll have to jump!'

Jenny and the other birds flew at the guards to try to distract them. Rosehip was flung aside and landed on a conveyor belt where candies were getting stamped in the shape of fruit. But when she tried to pull herself out, she found herself stuck to the sticky surface of the belt and progressing towards the stamping arms at an uncomfortably fast pace.

'Help!' she cried. 'I'm stuck!'

At any second, Rosehip would be stamped into the shape of a raspberry. But she was saved in the nick of time by Toadflax, who swooped down to rescue her. Seconds later he had to rescue Bud from a vat of chewing gum and

Speedwell from becoming the soft centres in a box of chocolates.

One of the guards was just about to grab Twill when, in one huge, superhuman leap, she jumped clear over the chasm! And just before the rough hands of the guard were upon him, Blake jumped, too. But he didn't quite make it. He grasped the edge of the greasy floor, his legs dangling into the dark chasm.

'Help me!' cried Blake.

'Hold on, Blake,' squealed Jenny, trying with the help of her friends to lift him out. But it was no use. They weren't strong enough.

Blake's fingers were very quickly sliding off the floor, slippery with candy grease, and to make matters worse, the other side of the floor was quickly coming to meet his.

'Oh, Jenny! Help! I can't hold on! I'm slipping! Help!'

'Well, that about solves our problem,' sniggered one guard to the other. 'We won't even have to tell the boss about this.'

'But we'll have to get rid of the other kid, too,' said the second one, indicating Twill.

'Yeah, that's right!' The first laughed, approaching Twill. 'Come on, curly, let's go.'

But the guard didn't know who he was dealing with. With one quick blow, Twill gave him a kick in the shin and a punch on the nose that sent him reeling over the edge of the floor and into the black pit.

'Harold!' shouted the other guard, looking down into the pit. 'Quick, boys, get a rope!'

The far side of the moving floor was only a few feet away. In a few moments the two sides would meet and Blake would fall and be trapped in a dark pit of poisonous gas. Twill looked over to Blake, clinging to the edge by his fingertips. Then with one quick movement, she grabbed him by his coat and threw him clear out of the chasm.

Jenny stared at Twill in admiration but then realised that guards were still all around them. They weren't out of the quicksand yet.

'Quick, run!' she cried.

With ten guards and factory workers chasing them, they just managed to escape out the door of the factory and across the parking lot into the woods beyond without being caught. But the pursuit didn't end there. As they continued their escape down the lumberjack trail, they could hear the revving of car engines behind them.

Suddenly, Jenny heard a loud crash behind her and when she looked back, she saw that Blake was gone.

'Blake!' she cried. 'Oh, not again!'

'I think he fell,' said Rosehip.

Jenny looked down the side of the trail and found it dipped straight down, dizzily down, into a deep ravine. Blake was sprawled at the bottom of it.

Jenny flew down, with Twill following, skidding and stumbling down the edge of the steep ravine. Her friend was lying on the dry forest floor amongst the leaves and brambles, quite still. His leg lay at a peculiar angle to the rest of his body.

In a flurry of wings, the other birds fluttered down the ravine.

'Methinks he fell over the edge of the ravine,' said Toadflax. 'He tripped over a root, a long coil of a root like a serpent.'

They heard the roar as the cars above them on the lumberjack trail passed by the spot where they were crouched, hidden, in the ravine.

'Blake!' cried Jenny, giving him a couple of not-so-gentle pecks on the cheek to try to rouse him. He didn't respond. 'Blake, wake up!'

But Blake didn't budge.

Chapter Seventeen

Jenny felt a sickness in her heart, a sickness which told her that her friend was beyond reviving.

'Jenny, what can we do?' said Peat.

'I-I will have to go for help,' she said numbly.

Jenny flew as fast as she could, following the lumberjack trail. The bright light of day was beginning to soften into evening. The shadows of the forest became long and black. She noticed that the trail began to look unfamiliar. Where was the old log cabin of Hermit's Pass? Jenny started to feel uneasy. She could no longer recognise anything along the trail. And the further Jenny flew, the darker and more forbidding the forest became. Every passing breeze set the leaves above her rustling with a sound like voices whispering. Voices seemed to come out of every shadow and corner, bubbling out of the forest stream and through the ferns and bracken.

'Jenny! Jenny, where are you?'

'Mother, is that you?' Jenny cried.

Another voice sounded like her father's. 'Jenny, what are you doing, girl? Why didn't you just come to me? You're too young to worry about stuff like this.'

'Father, where are you?' she cried. But there was no one at all, just her and the forest.

'Jenny, would you grow up!' came her sister's scornful voice. 'Turning into a bird. What a totally dorkish thing to do! But then that's what you are - a dork! And you always will be.'

'No,' cried Jenny, flying as fast as she could to try to get away from them. 'I can do this! You're wrong!' She felt tears stinging her little eyes. Soon the tears blurred her sight and she ended up crashing headlong into a fir tree. 'You're all wrong!' she squeaked, pulling herself out of the tree. She felt weary and sore.

'Jenny, we all love you,' said the voice of Jenny's mother. 'I know that your father and I are not the best parents but we do love you.'

There were so many voices now coming at her from every corner of the forest that Jenny felt dizzy. She just wanted to sink on to the cool forest floor and go to sleep. Maybe when she woke, it would all be over, like a bad dream. She started to close her eyes when she was startled by a noise coming from the trees above her.

Jenny watched a great black bird land on the bough of a cedar tree before her. He stretched out his tattered black wings and gave a loud caw that echoed through the forest. It was so loud and rough that it pierced Jenny's ears and made her shudder with fear and pain. The crow looked down at her, so small and helpless on the forest floor.

'At last I have found you, my dearest!' he

cooed in his deep, syrupy voice.

'Go away!' Jenny cried. 'My friend is dying. I must get help.'

'It's your fault Blake is dying,' said Professor Mennis the crow, swooping now to a bough of another tree and glaring at her from a fresh angle. 'Because you are so nosy. Jenny has to do something about the environment, Jenny has to be the hero. Jenny, Jenny, Jenny.'

As the crow repeated her name, it was echoed by the voices of a hundred people, whispering her name through the forests, chiding her and mocking her. She trembled with terror and when she tried to move her wings, she couldn't. They were frozen to her sides. 'Leave me alone,' she pleaded. 'I wanted to do something. I wanted to help.'

'But you had to drag everyone into it, too,' said Professor Mennis. 'Why don't you just leave things as they are and don't go sticking your nose in places where it doesn't belong? We own this world and there is nothing you can do about it.'

'There is something I can do,' she cried. 'There is! There is!'

Ahead of her, she could see a sparkle through the trees and realised she had been following a trail that hedged a lake. She didn't have to go very far before the trail came to a dead end. If she could just make it there, she knew she would be safe. She felt the strength come back into her wings, and just as the crow was about to dive upon her and swoop her up in his sharp claws, she flew out of his grips and down the trail and beyond.

The dead end opened up into a magnificent vista of a serene lake and mountains trimmed with evergreen trees and maples. The water was wonderfully calm and peaceful. The clouds were tinged with pink and gold and the sky was turquoise. Jenny was safe. When she had escaped the darkness of the forest, the crow had disappeared. Her heart was beating so hard she could hardly breathe, but she couldn't help but take a moment to take in the wonderful sight.

A man in a canoe had paddled round the bend of the trees. It was not unusual to see people canoeing on the lake, it was a very popular pastime. But who could claim to have seen a stone canoe? Yet one was being paddled towards her and at a great speed. The navigator, from what she could see, was dressed in a wonderful buckskin coat decorated with coloured beads and feathers.

Soon the canoe was upon her and she could see the face of the man. A wonderful face, a calm face, with fine features and dark eyes and long, tar-black hair plaited with beads. A face she had come to know so well.

It was Louis.

Chapter Eighteen

In one nimble hop, the navigator got out of his boat and pulled it up the little slip of beach before her. He did it with such ease that the stone canoe might as well have been made of styrofoam. It was carved with lively designs of woodland animals: bears and deer and foxes.

'Louis,' cried Jenny, 'Louis!'

Louis turned around and saw her sitting on the bulrush. She alighted on the prow of the stone canoe.

'I see you, little one,' he said. 'How is life treating you as a bird? Are you happy now?'

How did he know what had happened to her? It was days since she had seen Louis. He had seemed to disappear after that night he stayed for dinner. But how could he know?

'Oh, Louis, I'm miserable. My friend Blake has fallen into the ravine. I think he is dying. Can you help?'

The man she knew as Louis sat down on a stone and contemplated the little creature hopping up and down on the prow of his stone canoe. He took out a long, delicately carved pipe from a leather pouch around his waist. Into this pipe he poked tobacco and lit it with one quick flick of a flint on the stone he was resting on. He puffed away quietly, the smoke curling lazily into the rosy evening sky.

'Louis, please, you must help him. You have to come.'

When he was finished smoking, Louis put the pipe back into his pouch and stood up. He looked so grand and tall as he stood there in all his Indian finery that Jenny was momentarily taken aback. He was not the Louis that she knew. He was somehow even better.

'I am Glooscap,' he told her. 'And I can help you if you want it badly enough.'

'Glooscap?' said Jenny, confused. 'Louis, you are Glooscap?'

Jenny's mind raced. She remembered what Toadflax had told her. Glooscap was a young man who travelled the world, fulfilling wishes. He had the power to make things grow. He created all the animals and plants of the world. He was a god.

And seeing him standing there against a backdrop of the mountains and lake and the warm glow of the sunset, it was not difficult to believe.

'I am Glooscap of the trees, of the mountains, of all the creatures of these forests. I am Glooscap of the beginning and I am Glooscap of the end.' He turned to face the wonderful vista. 'I have come from the south to visit my birthplace in the north. I am very disappointed in what I see.'

Jenny stared, not knowing what to say. She had never met a god.

'How did you know who I was?' Jenny asked. But Glooscap wasn't listening to her.

'Here, stay on this prow,' he told her. 'I will take you to a land where there is no sickness or death, and you can tell me your wish again.'

So once more Glooscap launched his stone canoe and they glided into the calmness of the lake. Glooscap paddled the canoe, but not a sound was made from the movements of his paddle. Everything was peaceful and still.

Jenny peered into the lake from her perch and watched the trout and bass touring around the lake bottom. The canoe pushed through tall, flowing water grasses and cattails, and skimmed through beds of waterlilies. She marvelled how a stone canoe could stay afloat.

Glooscap said nothing as he paddled. Soon they came to an island. Here he pulled up his canoe on the grey, sandy shore. Jenny lifted her wings in flight, but at the very moment she left the canoe, a miraculous change took place and she found herself standing there as a human being, complete, all the bits exactly as she remembered them.

Jenny had never seen such a beautiful, natural place. Flowers grew out everywhere; wild Rosehip and lilies, irises and violets. Birds sang from every tree and the plants were a brilliant green and the soil rich brown as chocolate. The ferns curled and bent as they passed. Here the sun was not so hot and the air smelled sweet and fresh.

They walked through this splendour until they

came to a bubbling spring in a grotto. The spring jetted straight out of the earth and splashed down against the smooth stones beneath it. The water sparkled gold and silver, brilliant in the warm sun. All around the fountain, flowers grew and blossomed more brilliantly still. Where every droplet of water fell, a flower grew from the spot and burst instantly into bloom. A droplet fell before Jenny's feet and a lily sprang up and unfolded its purple petals before Jenny's eyes.

Jenny wanted more than anything in the world to take a drink of this water. It looked so clear, so refreshing and her mouth felt parched and dry, like a desert. Nothing but a sup from this would cure her, but Glooscap forbade her.

'Not from this spring,' he told her as he took from his satchel a leather waterskin. He filled it with the sparkling water of the spring. Then he replaced its stopper and put it back into his bag.

As they travelled through the woods, Jenny heard laughter and shouting and saw over a hedgerow of prickly thorns, the pointed tops and curls of smoke of a cluster of wigwams. A Micmac village. Jenny didn't think that Native Indians lived in wigwams any more. She was very curious and wanted to investigate, but when she turned around again, she saw that Glooscap had built a fire and was roasting a salmon on a spit. He had done all this in a matter of seconds!

When they had eaten the salmon - and Jenny had never in her life tasted better food - they sat looking at the fire. Jenny could see Louis through the leaping flames, smoking his long pipe. But then Louis began to transform and Jenny discovered that he really was Glooscap. Only a god could do what he did.

His first change was to the shape of a hare, leaping through the spitting flames. Then he changed again and became a great moose with antlers metres wide, bowing his huge, hoary head. Then Glooscap spread his arms wide so that the flames sprang up all around him, and he became a golden eagle, with sparkling wings, and then, in the cracking sparks which flew and floated in all directions in the air, Glooscap changed into a raccoon with piercing black eyes and twitching whiskers and a little hand which beckoned to Jenny through the flames.

Suddenly Jenny understood what was happening. All these animals she had seen at some time over the last few days, and they had all been Glooscap. The hare in her mother's delphiniums. The moose in the woods. The eagle that had attacked the crow on the telephone pole. The raccoon that led her to the factory. They had all been Glooscap. He had been there all along, guiding her and protecting her from danger.

Then his transformations were finished and Glooscap walked over to her, a man again.

'Jenny, you made a wish. You wanted to be a bird and fly away from everything. That wish came true. Now you are here as a person again.'

'So it was you and not my father's potion that turned me into a bird?' said Jenny, rubbing her eyes, which were stinging from the smoke.

'Yes. But once I grant a wish, that is all. It can not be undone. Once a man came to me and asked me to grant his wish to live to be very old. He wanted to be immortal but I couldn't do that.'

'And what happened?' asked Jenny.

Glooscap pointed to a very old, twisted tree, bowing low over the water. 'I turned him into a cedar tree and there he stands ever since.'

'Oh,' said Jenny.

'But I decided to grant you another wish. You see, Jenny, I thought you could help me,' said Glooscap. 'I don't like what is happening to this world, and I want people like you to help me. You have a lot to offer, Jenny, but you had a lot of anger to get rid of. Now, unlike that cedar tree, I'm giving you one last wish. Anything you desire. I can make you into a human again.'

'So, once I leave this island, I will become a bird again unless I wish to be a human?' she asked.

'Yes, that is true. But it is up to you to make the wish.'

'But I can make any wish I want?'

Glooscap nodded.

But Jenny didn't need to think. She wanted to have her own self back, but she knew there was something far more important she had to do.

'My wish is for you to save my friend, Blake.'

'Are you sure that is what you want to do?' asked Glooscap. 'Don't you want to be back to yourself again?'

'Yes, I want it more than anything!' she

exclaimed. 'I've learned so much in these past days about the world and about myself. There's so much I want to do. But I must save my friend or I will never forgive myself. You see, it's all my fault he is lying at the bottom of that ravine. I forced them all to go. I said it was their responsibility. I brought all my friends into danger.'

'You must be sure, Jenny, because once you make this decision, it can never be undone. You will never be the same again. You will be a bird until you die. You will never be able to be with you friends or your family again. Your life as a human will be over forever.'

'I know,' she told him. She looked one last time at her human form. She looked at her hands and flexed her fingers, and felt her face. She looked for the last time at her body as if she was saying goodbye to an old friend. But at the end of it all, there was still only one decision. 'You must save Blake.'

Glooscap took a large bough from the ground and lit it in the fierce flames of the bonfire. It sizzled into flame.

He launched the stone canoe and once again they slipped silently into the water. Jenny watched the island until it became blurred and indistinct in the weak light and then suddenly disappeared altogether, like a phantom into the mist of the lake. Night was almost upon them and the torch Glooscap held in one hand created a bight orange glow in the water.

As soon as Glooscap pulled the canoe to shore

again, Jenny took one step to land. She was a robin again. But she didn't give the transformation a thought, her attention was fixed on Blake's fate.

Soon Glooscap came to the place where Blake's body lay at the bottom of the ravine, Jenny's friends all around him.

Peat flew up to her at once. 'That didn't take you very long. We thought you'd be away for hours. You were only gone a few moments.'

A few moments? Jenny felt as if she had been away for hours.

Glooscap stuck his flaming torch into the earth. It crackled away as he opened his pouch and produced the leather waterskin he had filled in the fountain. He dribbled a little of the sparkling water over Blake's lips. Then Blake began to glow, as if he had a light inside him. The glow started at his head and travelled all along his body to his feet. When it had passed through his feet, Blake opened his eyes.

'Blake, Blake,' cried Jenny, coming to land beside him on the ground. 'How do you feel?'

'Oh, my head aches,' he moaned, slowly sitting up. There was a big red mark on his forehead. 'What happened?'

'A root rose up like a serpent before your feet and you were cast by its design through the air into the chasm where you nearly met Death at its bottom, or so legend has it,' explained Toadflax.

'You fell, fell, fell,' said Rosehip, landing on his shoulder.

'Glooscap,' said Jenny, but as she turned she

111

saw that he had gone.

'Who's Glooscap?' asked Blake, rubbing his forehead. 'Oh, that hurts.'

'Oh, nothing. I hiccuped,' said Jenny. 'Glooscup-glooscup.'

'I didn't know birds could hiccup,' Blake said as he got to his feet and shook the dirt and moss out of his jeans. 'You're right about one thing,' he said, emptying his sneakers of any offending pine needles. 'We'll have to tell the police about what's going on in that factory. They're on to us now.'

Chapter Nineteen

As Blake dashed out of her house, he nearly tripped over Jenny. She had been hopping impatiently on the doorstep. He took her in his hand.

'Well? Well?' she demanded. 'What happened? Did you phone the police?'

'Your mother had already phoned them. Your father didn't return today from the presentation at the television station, and she hasn't been able to get in touch with him. She thinks he was kidnapped.'

'Oh, no!' cried Jenny. 'Why is all this happening?'

'I told your mother about the factory. If your father was kidnapped, would they have taken him there?' asked Blake. 'It must be the factory. Where else could they hide him?'

'I've got to save my father,' exclaimed Jenny, taking off from Blake's hand.

'Wait!' he shouted. 'I'll come too!'

'No, no, I'm faster!' Jenny squeaked over her shoulder. 'You stay here and call the police and tell them what you know about the factory.'

She flew off as fast as her wings could take her to the Singing Tree where her friends were anxiously awaiting her return. Jenny had to take a second to catch her breath and then it all came out in a rush.

'Fa- Professor Wren's been kidnapped by men from the factory - I have to save him!'

'Professor Wren!' they gasped all together.

'Jenny, we'll come, too,' said Peat. 'All of us will come.'

'No, you can't! It's too dangerous. I don't want any of you to get hurt.'

'We have to come,' said Toadflax. 'Jenny, we've all learned a lot from you since you came to us. You opened our eyes. We want to help, we want things to change. Please, we've been with you this far, we want to be with you the rest of the way.'

They were soon high above the trees, past Jenny's shingled roof and into the thick forest. Speedwell the swallow used his good navigational skills and Toadflax used his sharp sight to find the factory, nestled in under the crest of a cliff on Kenwick Mountain. Jenny noticed that lots of other people had found it, too. It was surrounded by squad cars, their red lights flashing in the bright heat of the afternoon. She scanned the crowds of people for her father, but didn't see him. Her father had to be somewhere in that factory and it was up to her to find him.

Chapter Twenty

Jenny and her friends slipped in through the double glass doors when the last factory worker left, wearing a gas mask and with his arms raised over his head. It didn't take them too long to realise that the smell was the very same one they had encountered the last time they'd snuck into the factory. It was the fumes from toxic waste. The waste was leaking and the fumes had filled the factory! The birds split up to search the factory for Jenny's father. In a terrible panic, Jenny scouted the empty halls until finally she found her father, half-sitting, half-lying, in a chair in the office.

She landed on the arm of the chair and peered into his half-closed eyes. Her father was not looking his usual chirpy self. It was clear that the fumes had made their way into this office and that her father was suffering for it.

As if waking up from a daydream, he looked over to the table where he saw a little robin sitting on the stapler in front of him. He rubbed his eyes, as if it were an illusion. But the bird was still there, and when he looked around, several other birds had flown into the rooms too: an Acadian owl, a chickadee, a sparrow, a swallow and a redwinged blackbird. Oh, and another robin was sitting on the handle of a coffee cup.

'My life must be passing before me,' said Professor Wren to himself. 'That's what it is. Or it's a dream. It could be a dream.'

'Father, it's me,' Jenny squeaked, but her father only stared in amazement at her as she hopped up and down in front of him.

He looked down at the half-empty box of Acid Drops & Lollipops chocolate after-dinner wafers and pushed them away in disgust. 'I'm never going to touch these things again!' he vowed.

'Oh, Father, please understand me,' cried Jenny. The fumes were rolling in through the air vent on the wall.

'The air vent,' said Bud. 'That's where the poisons are coming through.' He and Juniper flew up, dragging Professor Wren's jacket from the shiny concrete floor. As they flapped their wings, they tried to stuff the jacket into the vent. But the fumes were too much for them. They fell to the ground and lay still.

Jenny tried one more time to get her father's attention, leaping up and down on the steel stapler and crying to him in her shrillest voice, but no matter what she did, her father just stared at her blankly, open-mouthed. She had to try to communicate with him. But how? Then she had an idea. She had learned Morse code from one of the camping trips her father had taken the scouts on. She could remember it very clearly herself because she had got great fun out of it with Blake afterwards, sending messages to each other by knocking their pencils against their desks, much to the great annoyance of their teacher, Mrs Boyle.

Just let me remember, she thought to herself, what is the code for Danger?

'Dot, dot, dot, dash,' Jenny pecked on the top of the table with her beak. 'Dot, dot, dot.'

Her father looked hard at her, furrowing his brows.

'Dot, dash, dot...'

'That almost sounds like Morse code,' her father exclaimed. 'I must be going crazy!' He listened a little longer, rubbing his stinging eyes. 'I am either delirious or this little robin is trying to tell me something. Let's see now: D-A-N-G-'

'Dot, dot, dot, dash, dash...'

'Danger,' her father said. 'Poison.' Suddenly her father opened his eyes wide and sniffed the air. 'Gases! That's it. That's what I'm breathing!'

Suddenly they were interrupted by a loud voice from a speakerphone.

'Anyone left in the building, please come out with your hands up!'

Professor Wren reached for the door but staggered backwards drunkenly. He held on to the side of the desk for support. 'Oh, my little friends, whoever you are ... uh ... I think these gases have gone to my head! Uh, what's that sound? That humming? The generators ... don't tell me they left them on!'

Professor Wren stumbled awkwardly through the door into the office next door where he found a touch-button phone. But the gas was growing

117

stronger and he couldn't coordinate himself to push the buttons to telephone the police headquarters. His aim was a little off and after a few tries, Jenny thought she'd better take over. She pushed 911 with her beak.

'Uh, thanks,' her father said, shaking his head in amazement. 'When I get out of this ... Uh, hello? Police? This is - uh - Leo Wren.'

'Professor?' Police Constable Kennedy's worried voice came over the phone. 'Where are you?'

'I - I was kidnapped. I'm in the Acid Drops & Lollipops factory in the mountains. They've been burying toxic waste and - and it has been leaking into Lake Omegod!'

It all made sense now. They obviously thought that Professor Wren had been photographing them rather than storks when he went to the lake that night. That's why his lab had been turned upside down. They must have been looking for the photographs. They must have kidnapped him either to threaten him to stop his campaign or to silence him.

There was the sound of sirens outside the factory.

'I know,' said the constable. 'We've made arrests. We're trying to evacuate the building. We've seen foreign ships coming into dock for some time now. When the boy, Blake, telephoned us last night with his story, it all just fitted together.'

'Blake?' Professor Wren wasn't sure if he'd heard him correctly.

'Yes, sir, Blake and your daughter - well, they'll tell you all about it. We've made arrests, but most of the workers seem to have deserted the operation before we got there.'

'Well, th- they must have left the generators on,' said Professor Wren. He was fading fast from the fumes and the receiver slipped from his hand. 'I can hear them.'

'Professor Wren! Professor Wren!' Jenny could hear the constable's voice crying excitedly from the phone.

Professor Wren grabbed the dangling receiver again.

'I - I'm still here,' he said. 'If those gases come in contact with any sort of heat, there could be a terrible explosion. It would be catastrophic! I - I have to try to turn them off.'

'I don't think that would be wise, sir,' said the constable. 'The best thing is to get out of there as soon as possible. We'll send over an emergency crew.'

'There's not enough time!' Professor Wren shouted angrily into the receiver. 'If this factory goes up, it will take half of this province with it and the whole countryside will be poisoned.'

'All right, Professor Wren. We have the factory manager here, he'll guide you, won't you, Mr Hawkings?'

'Yes, yessss.' Jenny heard the hissing voice of Sedric Hawkings.

Jenny's father staggered out of the office and on to the factory floor. It was completely empty. The levers that turned off the generators were clear over on the other side of the factory. Her father was almost crawling by the time he reached them. With his last ounce of strength, he turned them all off. All except one. He collapsed on the floor, unconscious.

Jenny, with the help of Peat and Toadflax, managed to pull the last one down. The lights and the noise of the generators went off. They were in silent darkness.

Jenny and her friends tried to haul her father out of the factory to safety. But her father was so heavy that the combined strength of a few little birds, weakened by the toxic fumes, wasn't going to be enough.

'Oh, Father,' she cried, trying to pull him by his shirt sleeve. 'Please don't die, please.'

If her father couldn't be saved, then she wasn't going to be either. But just as Jenny bent over her father, she saw two human hands. One look over her body was enough to tell her that she had been transformed back into her human form! Her friends stared at her in amazement.

Then, as if that wasn't enough, the ceiling started to part. They must have switched on that lever. Sunlight poured in from the ever-widening opening and a great flock of all kinds of birds, including storks and hawks, led by a grey owl, descended through it. Though her father wasn't conscious, he was at that moment getting the finest tribute of his career. The many claws of these birds took up her father's body and hoisted him high up into the air and out of the top of the factory, carrying him at last to safety.

'Go,' Jenny told her friends, who were still staring at her, stunned by her transformation. 'Get out before you're poisoned. I can find my own way out now.'

'I guess I should have known,' said Toadflax, flapping into the air. 'There always was something different about you, something special.'

'Goodbye, Jenny,' said Rosehip. 'See you on the other side!'

'Goodbye!' Jenny cried. 'Goodbye!'

Her friends, clutching the limp bodies of Bud and Juniper, swerved drunkenly up through the sunbeams and finally out to safety through the parting in the ceiling. Jenny hoped they would be all right and watched them until they were safely out of the factory.

The only one left now was Peat. He had remained behind.

'I guess there isn't any hope for us after all,' Peat told her, looking critically at her human form.

'Get out, Peat. Please!' she said, wiping the tears from her eyes. 'Please, I want you to get out safely.'

'I'll miss you,' he told her before he, too, flew into the misty air of the factory. As he was halfway to the top, he sang down to her. 'And I won't forget anything! You'll see, I'm going to give that Council a run for their money! One step for evolution! One step for birdkind!'

Jenny laughed weakly and brushed back her tears. Now it was her turn to escape. Her eyes were nearly popping out of her head for the stinging and she could hardly breathe, but she managed to find one of the worker's gas masks and dashed across the slippery floor towards the glass double doors of the factory. With one last heave, she was through the doors and to the safety of the fresh air beyond.

Before she got a chance to think, paramedics rushed to her side. Overhead, she could hear the sound of helicopters.

'I'm all right,' she told them, 'I'm OK now.'

But they made her sit down. They asked her where her father was, and Jenny looked across the factory grounds to where he lay, unconscious, where his bird rescuers had left him on the grass outside the parking lot.

Her mother, sister and brother rushed to her side.

'Jenny, we were so worried,' her mother cried, embracing her. She had been crying. 'You were there one moment and gone the next. Where's your father?'

He was being loaded into an ambulance. Jenny's family left to find out how he was.

'Jenny, is that you?'

It was Blake. He sat down beside her on the grass and put his hand on her shoulder, peering into her face with anxious grey eyes. He wasn't sure if it was Jenny or Twill.

She smiled wearily. 'Yes, Blake, It's me. I'm back to my old self.'

Chapter Twenty-One

It was the last day of March Break, and Jenny was spending it stretched out on the Chesterfield before her favourite soap opera. She had a can of 7-Up in one hand and a bag of cheese-coated popcorn in the other - all the necessary equipment for an afternoon of complete vegitude. After all, tomorrow was school again. She didn't really dread it as much as she'd thought she would. She had one good friend, and she was looking forward to seeing him.

The house was deserted that day, as it usually was, but Jenny didn't feel alone. The house seemed full of her family's life and personality, and she felt curiously at peace.

Her programme was interrupted with a newsflash.

'We would like to bring you a news update on the crisis on Kenwick Mountain. Through the bravery of Professor Leonard Wren, what could have been a great environmental catastrophe was prevented. Investigations have unearthed that toxic chemical waste was being illegally buried in Kenwick Mountain. Acid Drops & Lollipops, Inc., producers of a popular product range of sweets and breathmints, was the factory used as a front for this illegal and dangerous operation. Waste, shipped from over ten countries, was buried under the mountain, and this waste was leaking into our streams and rivers and polluting our lakes.

'And now, here is a clip from the recording of the speech given yesterday by our Premier at the World Wildlife Trust Conference, at which Professor Wren was the honorary guest.'

'It is through the effort and dedication of people such as Professor Leonard Wren,' said the Premier, 'that real progress can be made. We need people to take action and fight for what they believe in. Perhaps, with role models like Professor Wren, we can all in our own way make a difference. But we have a long way to go. It seems certain now that our climate is changing. CFCs have irreparably eroded the ozone layer and something has to be done quickly. Perhaps we can look to our next generation to really make a difference ...'

Jenny felt very proud of her father and how hard he worked for what he believed in. The fact that she didn't get any credit didn't bother her. She was just happy that Lake Omegod was saved. She knew that she, too, would have her chance.

In fact, there was one little difference she wanted to make at that very moment...

As if drawn by a magnetic force, she abandoned her soap operas and cheese-coated popcorn to go to the laboratory. Inside, she was confronted with the familiar squawking and singing of the residents. She went straight for Twill's cage.

'Jenny, Jenny,' cried Twill. 'Where have you been? I'm going nuts in here. Let me out, let me out!'

'That's just what I'm going to do,' she laughed as she opened the little wire door. In one hop, Twill was perched on the cage's threshold. 'I think I'm ready for it, now. I'm definitely ready. I can feel it, feel it. I'm ready. Don't hold me back, I'm going for it!'

Twill spread her little wings and in one fell swoop she was into the air. A little unsteadily at first, but then as surely as an arrow she flew through the screen door and into the great world beyond. 'Whoo-ee, no one can stop me now!' she cried as she flew.

Jenny hurried out after her. Outside the laboratory, she watched as her friend flew in a few circles around the front garden, testing her wings. Eventually, the robin came to rest on Jenny's favourite tree.

The Singing Tree was singing away merrily too, and now it had one more songster. Jenny knew that Twill would fit right in there. Jenny didn't go to the tree; she didn't want to disturb the birds that made it their home.

Just then, as if in a dream, Jenny saw a figure emerge through the plum and peach trees and walk towards her. It didn't take a moment to recognise the placid face that she knew could only belong to Louis or Glooscap, she wasn't sure which. He was dressed in ordinary clothes and his white lab coat, but he looked every bit as legendary as he had done on the island.

'I just came to say goodbye,' he told her.

'Louis, I am a person again,' she exclaimed, running across the garden towards him and clasping his arm. 'How did it happen? I thought I would never see my body again!'

'You've done well,' he told her, taking her by the shoulders. 'You walked through the forest and you confronted your ghosts, and at the end of the journey, you found your true self.'

He took a little package from his lab-coat pocket. It was a leather pouch like the one that had carried the magical water that had brought Blake to life. 'I brought this for you,' he said, pressing the pouch into her hands. 'Whenever you want to find your spirit guide, take out the things in this bundle.'

Jenny gently opened the leather strings that bound the bundle. From inside, she took three bright feathers tied together with beads. They were robin's feathers.

'Use your gifts to do something wonderful, Jenny,' he told her.

With those last words, Louis turned and started back into the forest.

'Louis, will I ever see you again?' she called after him, but he had already disappeared into the leaves.

She knew that though she would never see him, she would be hard pressed to forget him.

Basement Press hopes you enjoyed *Jenny Wren*. To help us improve the POOKA series for you please answer the following questions:

1. Why did you buy this book?

_____

_____

_____

2. Did you enjoy this book? Why?

_____

_____

_____

4. What do you think of the cover?

_____

_____

_____

5. Have you ever read any other books in the POOKA series? Which ones?

_____

_____

_____

If there is not enough space for your answers on this coupon please continue on a sheet of paper and attach it to the coupon.

Name:_____

Address:_____

_____

Age:_____

Please post this coupon to:
BASEMENT PRESS, 29 Upper Mount Street, Dublin 2, Ireland
Tel: (01) 661 6128 Fax: (01) 661 6176

POOKA

A new series of Ttrilling Tales of Adventure and Mystery
for 8 to 13 year old readers.

OUT NOW

Jenny Wren
by Angela O'Hara

Hotfoot
by Tom Richards

The Museum Mystery
by Tony Foster

COMING SHORTLY

Hotfoot II Lucky's Revenge
by Tom Richards

The Mountain Mystery
by Tony Foster

The Secret of the Silver Sea
by Jenny Reid

All at the price of £3.99 each

To make sure you are kept up to date with POOKA
information, why not send us your name and address for
our POOKA mailing list

NAME:_____

ADDRESS:_____

_____

PHONE:_____ AGE:_____